Murder Retires

Kate O'Rafferty

Library of Congress catalogue data:
Murder Retires / O'Rafferty, Kate
p.cm
Summary: a murder mystery in a retirement community on Florida's West Coast

ISBN: 9798593048691

[1. Murder Mystery—Fiction. 2. Retirees.]

ISBN: 9798593048691

Table of Contents

Chapter One:
Meet Me at the Mall

Peggy Murray finished her wonderful hot shower and toweled off. One of the things she loved about being retired was having her early morning swims in the warm, Florida sunshine rather than at the indoor pool in the local YMCA. She and Jack had recently retired to Florida, leaving cold winters and high taxes back in their New York homeland.

Peggy was a lifelong swimmer who never gave up on her morning swims, believing that was the key to her keeping her trim figure all these years, and she just loved to swim early in the morning. She dressed quickly and hurried out to the lanai where Jack had set up the coffee machine. She was surprised to see that Jack was still having his coffee.

"Jack? Aren't you playing golf this morning?" she said, bewildered for a moment because Jack usually left for golf shortly after she started her morning swims.

"We have a later tee time today and I thought we could have breakfast together. You look like you're in a rush. Are you going somewhere?" Jack said.

"I'm going to the Santervas Mall to do some shopping. The snowbird going away dinner is tonight in the clubhouse," she said. "I need something to wear. I just haven't gotten the knack for dressing down here."

"You've never had a problem dressing before." Jack said.

"I know, but all I ever did was dress for the weather. Now I have to learn how to dress like a Floridian. You know," she took a breath, "you don't just wear summer clothes if it's warm. You have to dress for the season as well as the weather. Like now, it's March, and I would be looking for my lighter weight wools and jackets in New York. But here," she looked at the ceiling, "I think it's warm enough for what I call summer clothes, but they need to look more like winter light-weights. You know what I mean?"

Jack smiled and reached for a donut. "Of course I do," he said and reached for his copy of the *Wall Street Journal.* "I didn't realize it was such a problem."

Peggy laughed. "I know. You think I'm a little batty, but I haven't really learned to be a Floridian yet. See you later," she said and walked to the door of their retirement condominium.

Jack called after her. "Be careful at that mall, honey. I've heard some disturbing stories about it lately. You never know who's lurking in a place like that. It's almost deserted."

"Okay. I'll be careful. Radley's is still open. I'll watch my back."

Jenna Rivers drove her sporty little red car into the Santervas Mall in Bradenton, Florida.

She was very familiar with this mall, although she had only recently moved to Bradenton from Georgia. She was a native of Bradenton, having been born and bred in this city on Florida's gulf coast.

This mall was a good place to have a rendezvous. Very few people really went here anymore. It once had medium to high-end stores as tenants, but many of them had left the mall. The story was that teenagers were looting the stores in daylight and many customers were afraid to shop there. Another story was that the owners of the mall had other plans for the property. Either way, it had become a good place to go if you didn't want to run into someone who might know you. Usually.

Jenna very happily left Bradenton after her high school graduation to attend nursing school in Georgia, where she had won a scholarship. She didn't have any friends in her home-town and was looking forward to a new life. Her first marriage to Billy Bob Mason was a trial since Billy Bob liked to drink and get fired from his many jobs. Jenna finally had enough of the once handsome roguish man she'd been married to for twenty-odd years. The wreck of her own professional life was the final straw.

She, once more, wanted a totally new life, not a life in which she worked long hours for ungrateful people; a life spent just supporting her drunken husband. Again, she laughed, remembering how angry his sister was at her when she divorced him. What about your vows, you witch, she had called after her when they were leaving the courthouse. She left him with nothing but the clothes on his back.

The Watcher followed her. Aren't you the chic sophisticate, Jenna Rivers. Your time is almost up. Kiss Kiss.

The divorce was quick. No longer Mrs. Billy Bob Mason, Jenna embarked on a new career, a career which would open up the nursing home population to her charms. She had lost her medical license but she knew how to solve that problem. Using her maiden name, Wagner, Jenna trained as a CNA, a certified nursing assistant, having taken a twelve-week course in Georgia.

Always a planner, Jenna intended to work in an elite retirement/elder long-term care facility and find herself a wealthy and elderly widower, preferably with an incurable ailment.

She was very successful in her goal, and as Mrs. Walter Rivers, she had returned to her "native land". Her new husband, Walter Rivers, reluctantly agreed to leave Georgia for his new wife. He had become so very dependent on her.

Jenna was a trim five foot three woman in her early fifties. She carried her age very well. Her frosted blonde hair was cut stylishly short in a feathery style and her lightly tanned face complemented her large hazel-brown eyes. Jenna knew her best feature was her brilliant smile, which she was expert at flashing in a moment's notice, if there was a suitable male around.

He was a skinflint, but Jenna knew how to make the most of what was available to her. As his health deteriorated, Walter's hold on his assets was loosening, despite his tightwad habits.

Mrs. Walter Rivers dressed stylishly, expensive-conservative, as befitted her status as an upper-class matron, married to a wealthy retiree. As she strode into the mall, her red linen pantsuit by Chanel belied Jenna's couturier past. She had arrived and her wardrobe attested to it.

Humming her favorite song to herself (ironically, it was *When the Saints Go Marching In*) she alighted from her little car and walked briskly into the near-vacant shopping center. The handicapped license plate on the rear of her new and expensive little car afforded her one of the best parking spaces in the large and near-empty parking lot. Jenna's husband, Walter Rivers, was, indeed, handicapped, what with Parkinson's and early-onset Alzheimer's.

Glancing back at her car in the handicapped space, she couldn't help but laugh a little at the handicapped license plate. As if Walter could climb in or out of my car, she thought, delighting in the parking convenience his illnesses afforded her.

As she walked briskly away, an elderly woman using a cane, watched her and shook her head in obvious disapproval.

Another point for Jenna's amusement was the awe she had inspired in her teachers during her twelve week CNA training. They couldn't imagine how anyone could pick up and learn the material so quickly. Jenna was amused at this, since she actually could have taught the course if she hadn't lost her medical license. The one "accidentally" transposed number of her social security card insured her a new life with no connection to her former career. She presented herself as a stay-at-home wife in pursuit of a little career.

It was in the nursing home, as planned, that she met the perfect husband. Walter Rivers was a tall man, a wealthy man, and a divorced man. Young, and good looking, in his early sixties, Walter was suffering from the early-onset of Alzheimer's. As their relationship flourished, she was able to take him on outings and he seemed to be improving under her careful tutelage.

She didn't know about the Parkinson's at the time he proposed, but she did know he had one daughter from whom he was estranged. He told her about Barbara during their brief courtship and that he hadn't spoken to her for years. She did not forgive him for divorcing her mother and had accused him of having many affairs. He confided in Jenna that it was his wife who was unfaithful but he didn't want to share that information with Barbara. He became very agitated at the memory as he confided his pain to his indifferent but consoling care-giver.

Jenna was a little unsettled about his having a daughter, no matter how many years he'd not talked to her, but she knew she could handle her if it came to that.

As his illness progressed, she would take complete charge of him and his assets. She had wisely refused a pre-nuptial agreement, feigning insult and religious objections to such an arrangement. After all, how could you make a vow until death do you part if you were providing for divorce at the marriage's beginning? The weakened Walter Rivers did not insist. He was becoming totally dependent on his care-giver/fiancée.

Just in case the daughter came back into the picture, Jenna settled that possible problem easily enough. Immediately after the wedding ceremony, she took herself and her new husband to Bradenton, her turf. No one in Bradenton knew what she'd been doing since leaving right after high school, and Walter certainly had no ties there. All that her old classmates or neighbors knew was that she'd won a scholarship to a nursing school in Georgia.

Her mother never mentioned Jenna's marriage to Billy Bob Mason nor her only child's ill-fated career. She was never close to her mother and never confided in her. Her mother didn't even know that Jenna had become a doctor.

Now she had returned to Bradenton as Mrs. Walter Rivers. Most of the people she'd known didn't even question how long she was married to Walter Rivers. The few who remembered her assumed she'd been married to Walter for many years. They did admire how devoted she was to be taking care of her ailing husband. She was heroic in their eyes.

Most of the women Jenna knew when she was young had one thing in common with the women she met when she moved into the Sea Grass

Condominium Complex with her new, ailing husband. In spite of admiring her devotion to her husband, they all disliked her, but couldn't really tell you why.

She was aware of their feelings for her. She thought about it briefly and decided that she couldn't care less.

As Jenna strode through the outer door of the air-conditioned mall, Barbara Rivers Smyth let herself out of a beige, rented economy car and began to follow her into the mall, keeping back so she wouldn't share the door with her. Even though they'd only met briefly, Walter's daughter didn't want to confront her father's bride just yet.

Barbara looked around and noticed that this mall wasn't very crowded. The lack of people to shield her would make following her father's wife difficult. She noticed that most of the stores in the mall were closed. That would account for the lack of shoppers. She kept her distance, wondering what was going on in this place.

She'd only seen her father's wife once, and that was very briefly. One of the nurses at the nursing home had contacted her to tell her that a new nursing assistant had taken a very serious interest in her father and she thought she would want to know about it.

When she'd arrived at the home to see what was going on, the assistant nurse, Jenna Wagner, was just settling her father in his bed for the night. She'd introduced herself to Jenna, who nodded to her and swiftly ushered her out the door of the well-appointed suite, and into the hallway, insisting that she didn't want her patient to become agitated. Jenna explained that he'd been given his medications and needed to go to sleep.

Barbara was inwardly still angry with herself for letting Jenna get away with that little act. The next thing she knew her father had married this woman and left the state. The nursing home said they'd tried to warn her but that there was nothing they could do. And so, Barbara Rivers-Smyth had hired a detective agency to locate the newlyweds, and had taken up residence in a nearby hotel, watching and wondering what to do to help her ailing father.

The last anchor store in this part of the mall was Radley's Department Store. Barbara watched from behind a potted palm tree near the entrance to the store as Jenna rushed ahead into the doorway of the store and into the arms of a tall, well-tanned silver-haired man, who greeted her by lifting her off her feet as he kissed her again and again.

Barbara became infuriated and shouted, "You tramp! Married for three months to my poor father and having an affair while he's alone and dying."

The few people passing by stopped and stared at the tall, well-dressed brunette who was shouting at the loving couple embracing in the store's entrance.

Jenna and her loving friend parted for a moment. Then, Jenna's face broke into her huge smile. She started to laugh out loud, and hands on hips, she said, "No one cares, Barbara. Why don't you go back to Georgia where you belong! There's nothing for you here. He's not alone, if it's any of your business. I'm his primary care-giver and I don't care to deal with you. In fact, I don't want you visiting him. You'll upset him. Bye."

Seeing that her friendly male partner was inching away, Jenna turned her back on Barbara and rushed to catch up with him, taking his arm in hers, possessively, and they walked away.

 Barbara stood still, tears running down her face. The small group of shoppers looked away as if embarrassed and sorry for her.

She took a deep breath and managed to control herself. She walked out to her very beige car and sat, watching Jenna's car intently.

The watcher smiled again. Now, I see, another one on your list. How many, Jenna? How many?

Peggy Murray, recording secretary of the Board of Sea Grass Condominiums in Bradenton, shook her head at the spectacle she'd just witnessed.

I wonder who that woman is who was yelling at Jenna Rivers? she thought. She's so upset!   And what was Jerry Sands doing with Jenna? They're looking a little too cozy.

The salt and pepper-haired woman shook her head as she walked out of the mall, two shopping bags in hand, toward her mid-sized red SUV. Distracted by her thoughts about the strange scene she'd just witnessed, Peggy became very annoyed when she got to her car.

Someone had parked too close again, one of Peggy's pet peeves. I'll bet I have a few dings from this beauty. Whoever it is doesn't know how to park a car, she thought, looking at the doors of her car. No way would she be able to get into the driver's door. How am I going to squeeze into my car? She made a mental note to hate bucket seats which prevented her from getting in the passenger door and sliding over. These thoughtless people, she fumed. She couldn't park inside her own space but had to go over the lines!

An elderly woman using a cane approached the offending car, got in, and pulled out, solving Peggy's dilemma. Peggy didn't see any damage to her car and, being thankful for that, she got into her car and also drove away.

On her way home, Peggy mentally ran over the things she still had to do. The complex was having a pot-luck dinner party in the clubhouse tonight to bid the snow birds farewell until next winter. She had been assigned to bring hors d'oeuvres.

They'll be going home, their real homes, to see their real friends, she thought, a realization that she wasn't happy about being a part-time friend. A new Floridian who had forsaken her own home in New York, she had come here determined to be a real Floridian. Meeting up with others still tied to their homelands wasn't what she expected. Oh, well, she thought. I'll deal with it. I'll bring shrimp cocktail. I'd better stop at the store and buy some frozen shrimp so I have time to defrost it.

Jenna told Jerry she'd meet him at Sea Grass. They were taking their own cars back home. She got into her little red sports car and pulled out of the mall's parking lot.

The Watcher smiled to herself. Time is running out, Jenna. Should it be you or your husband? We'll wait and see. You didn't miss the first one. Oh, I forgot, you divorced him and I didn't know.

Barbara Rivers-Smyth started her car and followed two cars as they left the parking lot of the almost empty mall. She knew the little red one was Jenna's. Maybe the other one is her boy friend's, she thought. Finally, all three pulled into the parking lot of the Sea Grass Condominium Complex. Although the property was fenced, it did not have a forbidding gate. The two-building complex had several guest spots and Barbara parked as easily as if she belonged there. Jenna parked in her father's spot.

A third car moved slowly into the parking lot, slipping easily into a designated space.

The two lovebirds walked hand-in-hand toward the building on the north side of the pool and clubhouse, both of which were located between the two condo buildings in the complex. The buildings were brilliant white stucco with aqua trim, looking very Floridian.

They walked into the farthest building and entered the elevator. He pushed the button for the second floor.

Barbara followed, stealthily, using cars and landscaping to hide. She watched them wait and enter the elevator, and the electronic indicator next to the button showed that it stopped on the second floor.

She ran to the stairs next to the elevator and easily climbed to the second floor. Fortunately for her, she was in time to see the two putting a key into the lock on a corner unit a few steps from the elevator.

That was the last straw for Barbara. She openly approached Jenna and Jerry. "I'm not going to stand by and watch you make a fool of my father." Barbara held up her cell phone. "I've video-taped your escapade today and I will use it to have your marriage annulled. You are a pair. I'm sure your companion here is also married so I'm sure his wife would like to know about his activities."

Jenna turned furious eyes on Barbara. "Go peddle your wares somewhere else, Barbara. I'm going to sue you for harassment. Leave me alone!" she fairly growled.

With that the door to the unit opened wide and a tall, beautiful woman threw it aside. "What is going on here?" she demanded.

Jerry looked stunned. "What are you doing home, Kathryn," he demanded. "I thought you were at a tennis match. Your car isn't in its spot! I agree, what is going on here?" he ended.

"The match was cancelled and my car is in for service. That doesn't answer the question I asked. What is going on here?" Kathryn said in her low, almost musical voice.

Jenna hurried away, running into the elevator, which, fortunately for her, was still on the second floor. Barbara backed away toward the staircase, shocked at being in such a scene.

Jenna hurried to her building, the Manatee. Barbara continued to follow her.

Jerry shrugged his shoulders. "I ran into Jenna at the mall and that woman was following her. She was afraid to go home to let the woman find out where she lived so I stayed with her and then the woman came out of the stairwell and started shouting.

The Sands went into their unit together.

Veronica Davies knocked on her next door neighbor's door. She opened it a crack and called inside, "Hello. I'm your new neighbor. Anybody home?"

Walter Rivers made his way to the door using his walker, happy that someone was there.

He was having a good day. "Hello. Please come in. I'm Walter Rivers," he said, ushering his new neighbor inside.

Veronica was a little stooped with white hair and very lively blue eyes. She smiled at Walter. "I just moved in next door and thought I'd stop in to introduce myself. I hope I'm not imposing."

"No, no," Walter said as he sat down in his recliner. "My wife's not home but I'm sure she'll want to meet you."

Then he looked startled and sank back into another world, a world of silence.

Veronica smiled at Walter. A retired nurse, Veronica recognized the symptoms of both Alzheimer's and Parkinson's. "Have you had dinner?" she asked gently, her professional instincts coming back to her.

He shook his head and looked down at his hands. "Hungry." was the only word he uttered.

Veronica got up and walked into the kitchen looking for something to prepare for him.

She shook her head and walked back to Walter, carrying a tray of prepared food for him. She bent down to help him eat his food.

The door suddenly opened. Jenna stormed into the room. "Who are you and what are you doing in my house?" she snarled.

"I'm your new neighbor, Veronica Davies, and I found your husband hungry and sad," Veronica said. "I just came over to introduce myself. I'm sorry if I upset you." Veronica stood up and reached for her cane.

Jenna's disposition seemed to change immediately. "I didn't mean to be rude," she said. "I was just startled to find someone here. Thank you for fixing Walter's dinner for me. I was stuck in traffic while I was trying to get home to him."

Walter just stared at her.

Jenna walked Veronica to the door. "Nice meeting you." She said, looking at her watch.

Ignoring Walter, Jenna walked to the kitchen and took a covered dish from the refrigerator. She looked at the clock on the wall and started to walk briskly to the door. No time to change my clothes, she grumbled to herself. I'll have to get to that potluck supper right away to see if Kathryn is going to start anything. I am at their table and I don't want her to create a problem for me. I wonder where Barbara is.

Time's up, dear Jenna. Who will care? Nobody, as far as I can see. Problem solved. The Watcher was pleased.

Chapter Two:
Snowbird's Farewell Dinner

Peggy managed to squeeze her groceries and shopping bags into her denim lined shopping cart. This is the best thing I've gotten since I'm down here she thought. She was used to her attached garage back in Brooklyn, which made unloading her car very easy. Now she needed a cart to get from the car, in her designated parking space, to the elevator and finally into her apartment, or as they all called their apartments down here, their units.

Jack was home from his golf game. As she struggled in the door with the cart and her pocketbook, she realized Jack had invited Herb Anderson in for an après golf drink.

The two men were engrossed in a "car discussion". They were raving about some car in the parking lot that was the living end!

"Who do you think owns that GT?" Herb said, obviously admiring something called a GT.

Jack answered quietly as though he too was an admirer of a GT. "It cost someone, a few extra dollars. Those things start at over sixty grand."

"I could use a hand here, Jack, unless you're more interested in four on the floor than eating tonight," Peggy said remembering the expression designating manual transmissions from her youth.

"No way," Herb said. "This baby has six on the floor."

"Are you sure?" Jack said. "I heard they'd made an automatic transmission in the new models."

"Not this one," Herb said. "That car out there is the Shelby GT 350. No way would they put an automatic tranny in that baby."

Peggy finished putting the food away. She was thinking that she really didn't think having a car that's price started at over sixty thousand dollars was in her field of interests. The two shopping excursions left her tired and irritable.

I really wish I didn't have to go out tonight, she thought, but I'm on the food committee.

The clubhouse looked beautiful. It was early spring in Florida and the weather was perfect. The sometimes chilly nights were coming to an end. Days were becoming warmer. The room was decked out in fresh flowers, white table- cloths, gleaming crystal glassware and candle sticks with the new battery-operated fake candles. There was a three-piece band playing pop tunes and people were dancing.

Jack didn't feel well so Peggy Murray came alone, tired and looking forward to leaving as soon as she could. She looked around, trying not to attract anyone's attention so as not to get involved in a long conversation. Suddenly, Kathryn Sands, Mrs. Jerry Sands, stood up, picked up her evening bag from the table, and walked swiftly out the door.

She was a stunning woman. She was tall, had beautiful, thick shoulder length hair, and even features. She was a former model and it showed in her walk and carriage. Kathryn's demeanor, as she left the clubhouse, was subtly angry.

Peggy's eyes roamed around the table. There was Jerry Sands, husband of Kathryn, returning from the dance floor and pulling a chair out for Jenna Rivers, still dressed in the red linen pantsuit she'd had on at the mall that afternoon. I guess they had a nice dance, Peggy thought. She looked at the couple settling themselves at the table, obviously not noticing that Kathryn was no longer sitting next to her husband's empty chair. Now, Kathryn's chair was empty.

Not meaning to be staring, Peggy, nonetheless, noticed Jerry spill something into Jenna's glass. What is he doing? she thought, momentarily. Her thoughts were interrupted by Mable Milano, who rushed up to her.

"Peggy! Come quick! Miss Claudia demanded to be allowed to help in the kitchen and has started a fight with Bessie. I'm afraid she's going to hurt someone." Mable fairly shrieked.

"I'll try to talk to her. See if you can find Ralph. She sometimes listens to him." Peggy said.

Ms. Claudia was an eccentric woman in her mid-fifties. She had come to this complex part of a married couple, Mr. and Mrs. Jim Robbins. Shortly after they'd moved in, Jim had a heart attack and died, and, Claudia stopped taking her meds.

She was a nice looking middle-aged woman, who happened to be a schizophrenic. Sometimes she was a holy terror. In the beginning of her episodes the community tolerated her behavior, but, after a few physical episodes, they started looking into getting her evicted.

Her sons lived in California and made sure her bills, including her HOA fees were paid, which made it almost impossible to get her out of the complex.

As it turned out Ms. Claudia was teasing "the girls" as she called the volunteers who ran the social activities. They wouldn't let her help so she tormented them whenever she could. The furious food committee ordered her out of the kitchen, telling her, in no uncertain terms, that she was not welcome to be a volunteer.

Peggy watched as Ms. Claudia sulked out the door of the dining room that connected to the pool deck. What is she carrying? It looks like an old tee shirt. Ms. Claudia has a wicked look in her eyes, Peggy thought.

No one appears to be watching me, she thought, so I'll make my exit now. As she passed the pool deck she saw someone moving out there. Jenna and Jerry were having a romantic and private slow dance on the pool deck.

I wonder what Kathryn will think when she hears about this. She won't hear it from me, but the whole gossip posse is inside and I'm sure someone will report this dance to her.

That looks like Claudia rushing into the building, she thought. I hope I don't run into her in the elevator.

Claudia lived one floor above Peggy and Jack Murray.

No more watching, Jenna. Your time has run out. Time's up. Time to pay your debt.

The rifle was lifted over the railing and one shot rang out. No one heard it because of the music in the clubhouse. The shooter was an excellent shot.

Peggy stopped briefly, thought she'd heard something, and went directly to the elevator. I am so tired tonight. I can't wait to get a hot shower and into bed. She looked at the clock. I can't believe it's way past midnight, nearly two A.M!

Chapter Three:
The Lady in the Lake

Peggy Murray looked at the wall clock on her way out of the condo she and Jack bought as their retirement home. Their "Unit" she thought, amused at apartments being referred to as units.

It was almost eight o'clock. She was hurrying down to the pool deck so she could get her eight o'clock swim in. She was unsettled because of the stress between herself and her best friend, Gracie.

She did her best thinking as she swam her laps in the empty pool. Her conscience was somewhat bothering her. She knew down deep that she had caused the rift between them when she accepted the office on the Board.

It was such a cold March. It's not supposed to be this cold in South Florida in March, Peggy Murray thought, almost angrily, as she approached the pool for her daily early morning swim.

Peggy was about five foot three inches tall with a petite frame. Her once black, curly hair was now streaked with silver as she approached her late fifties.

Jack, her one and only love and husband of thirty years, was a few years older than she was and had asked her to retire when she turned fifty-five the previous year. Jack was an avid golfer and a successful accountant who was tired of New York's winters and taxes.

Peggy, a New York City high school English teacher, was eligible to retire at age fifty-five and so she did. Like two peas in a pod, Jack and Peggy loved each other and made each other happy.

Peggy loved to swim, especially in the early morning. That's when she organized her day mentally and sorted out the things that needed sorting in her new retired life. She hadn't yet been able to quiet the nagging feelings accosting her peace ever since the Pool Heater War.

Her towel and robe over her arm, Peggy rushed out her door and headed for the stairs. She'd rather run down the four flights of stairs to the pool deck than wait for the elevator. As she stepped onto the deck, a cold blast of wind assaulted her and she shivered involuntarily.

Peggy stood on the deck of the Sea Grass Condominium Complex Pool this beautiful but cold-for-Florida, March morning. Determined to get her morning swim regardless of this ridiculous weather, she walked over to the chair closest to the pool steps. She dropped her bag and her fuzzy pink robe, her towel and her pool slippers, onto the chair. Now prepared for when she was ready to leave the heated pool, she could grab her towel and robe immediately, before that cold wind careening over the lake could freeze her to death.

Peggy kept to routines to the point that Jack had started to call them rituals. "What would happen if you went to the pool at eight fifteen instead of eight o'clock sharp?" and "The world will not end if someone parks accidentally, once, in one of our parking spaces, or worse, over the line encroaching into your spot." Jack reminded her, laughing good-naturedly at his wife's pet peeves.

Peggy headed to the pool and she stopped abruptly, looking down at wet footprints leading out of the pool. Who could have gotten into the pool ahead of me, she wondered, half-aloud, as she surveyed the pool waters to see who was in the pool, hoping maybe Gracie was joining her.

The pool was empty. She shrugged her shoulders and entered the pool.

Aaah, she breathed out loud as she dipped under the very heated waters of the pool. That was a battle, she remembered triumphantly, the now infamous Pool Heater War, as the warm waters covered her up to her shoulders.

Peggy called the people who opposed the pool heater, "Polar Bears" behind their backs, of course. Those Polar Bears from Illinois and Michigan, not to mentions the Canadians, she laughed to herself, are obviously annoyed at having lost that battle. They were the famous snowbirds from the frigid north, who travelled to Florida each winter!

They were always arguing against turning on the pool heater. And, these days, they were almost a majority in the condo Association. According to the "Original Owners" side of the battle, these last few years the newcomers had started coming down earlier, some right after Labor Day, and they stayed longer, some into May. The Original Owners had aged since the complex was new and they were living there full time. They had developed a proprietary attitude and believed the newcomers were pushy.

As she floated on two of the complexes purple noodles, those Styrofoam noodle-shaped floating devices, she relived the pool heater battles.

What kind of people are opposed to turning on a pool heater? They were People from Michigan, Chicago, Wisconsin, maybe Massachusetts and, of course, Canada. They liked to show off how tough they were, Peggy thought, smiling at the memory. After all, they came from cold climates. But I looked up Michigan, she said out loud to no one. It's no colder than New York. Did I go around demanding people freeze in the pool because New York gets cold in the winter? No.

I didn't come to Florida so I could freeze to death because of the Polar Bears! She was even friends with some of them, sometimes. However, after she led the pro pool heater side of the battle, she noticed, some of them had gotten a little chilly toward her, even snubbing her on the pathways or while bobbing in the pool on the noodles. Peggy's daughter, Marissa, while visiting, said the pool looked like a big bowl of soup with dumplings bobbing on the colorful noodles.

Peggy's daughter's name wasn't really Marissa. It was Mary. Her father had started to call her Marissa as if it was the diminutive for Mary when it was actually the diminutive for Maris. No matter, the name stuck, except for her legal documents like driver's license or diplomas.

Ha, she thought as she let go of her purple noodles and started to swim her daily laps. I really got to them when I told them they should stay up north if they liked the cold so much. After all, in Coney Island, the Polar Bear Club goes into the Atlantic Ocean every Sunday from November to April.

Then there's the Greek Orthodox celebration of Epiphany on January's Orthodox Christmas. When the priest throws a golden cross into the icy waters of the Hudson River around Battery Park, young men dive into the frigid waters to retrieve the cross. Peggy shivered at the very thought of diving into the Hudson River at all, much less in January.

After that speech, Peggy smiled, remembering the meeting where she won the vote to keep the heater on if the temperature dipped below eighty degrees.

No one wanted to compete with the Polar Bear Club or the brave Greek young men. That's not why they had retired to Florida. Maybe she shouldn't have taken a bow when her side won the vote.

Maybe she shouldn't have accepted the position of recording secretary at that same meeting. Carried away by her success at winning the pool heater war, when the group that supported her, The Original Owners, put her into the position as an officer of the board by acclamation, she accepted the position that her best friend had been running for, unopposed.

Now Gracie was actually Peggy's former best friend. Now she had it solved, the nagging problem that kept her unsettled these past few days. She shouldn't have accepted the position on the board that her friend was running for, and she knew it.

So I lost a friend, she admitted. I'll apologize to Gracie. Maybe I can resign and try to give her the position. She turned on her back before leaving the empty but warm pool, and backstroked over to the handrail on the steps.

She owned the pool from eight AM until around ten when the dumplings, as Marissa called the noodle bobbers, came into the pool with their hats on, prepared to dish the dirt. "Have you heard" and "what do you think happened?" were favorite conversational openings. They were also known as the gossip posse, of late, led by none other than Gracie Anderson of Illinois. They had been good friends, Peggy thought wistfully.

I never should have accepted that office, she said regretfully to herself, remembering how nice it used to be when she and Gracie would have coffee in the mornings after their early swim. While their husbands played golf most mornings, Gracie used to go with her for her eight o'clock swims. Now she went alone.

The guys still played golf.

Peggy was from Brooklyn and was used to having many friends. She'd started to make new friends when she and Jack retired to Florida. They had decided not to be snowbirds but to be real year-round, genuine Floridians. Then they found out that the people they were making friends with in Florida were, indeed, returning to their real homes every spring. Probably to their real friends too, Peggy thought, suddenly missing her old friends and the fall, one of her favorite seasons in her homeland.

She steeled herself from homesickness. I'm too old for homesickness, she frequently told herself whenever the feeling swelled inside her. She was determined to be a Floridian and not a snowbird, like her new friends.

This seemed to make a difference between them and their new friends, at least to Peggy. She and Jack had abandoned New York, but their new friends had not abandoned their homelands. These people were still Michiganders or Canadians. They were, at best, part-time friends. Not what the Murrays were used to, they came and went and lived other lives. Jack, a retired accountant, adapted to their new milieu, but Peggy struggled to understand it. She felt, somehow, diminished, and lately, lonely.

Oh well, she didn't come down here to freeze to death. She had to lead that fight against a cold pool, or as they euphemistically called it, a crisp and refreshing pool, even if she did lose some of her new friends. She really didn't want to be "on the board". That was Gracie's goal, she remembered regretfully.

"Maybe I'm having trouble adjusting to retirement?" she said to no one.

The polar bears shouldn't think they could push a Brooklyn girl around, she said to herself as she climbed out of the warm water, ran to her huge towel and wrapped herself in it to sop up the dripping. Then she enveloped herself in the great pink robe waiting for her on her lounge. Now she was ready to thwart that cold wind coming off the lake, the beautiful lake that had drawn her and Jack to this complex.

Slipping her feet into her pool slippers, Peggy pulled her robe closer to her chilly body and walked over to the fence that surrounded the pool. It was a six-foot high chain link fence with two locked gates, controlled by electronic passes only given to owners at the rate of one per household. One gate was near the entrance to the clubhouse, the other at the rear end of the pool, nearest the lake. The pool overlooked the lake at that far end.

Peggy walked over to the back end of the pool to look out at the lake. A favorite ritual of hers, she liked to look at the water, even as it rippled with the wind crossing it on its way to the pool deck. She watched to see if birds flew down to catch a fish, or, if ducks swam by. She also looked for the occasional alligator. She liked to look out on a windy day, like this day, almost defying the wind and feeling very healthy and strong.

Now she gasped, loudly, and the gasp grew into a scream as she realized she was looking at a body floating face down in the murky waters of the lake, floating near the shore. It was a very well-dressed body, dressed in a bright red Chanel pantsuit.

Chapter Four:
Breaking the Rules
of the Complex

Peggy ran, screaming, to her bag on the lounge and reached inside for her cell phone. She always took her phone with her to the pool, especially when she was alone. She had tripped once and had to call Jack because her knee was bleeding profusely and she didn't think she could get upstairs without leaving a trail of blood behind her.

She dialed nine-one-one and calmly told the operator what she saw and the name of the condominium complex. She was thinking rationally now and thought she might see if maybe the woman in the lake could be helped. She dialed Jack but his phone went right into voice mail so she headed towards the rear gate to see if she could get down to the lake shore, wondering how she would pull the woman out of the murky lake water. The gate was open! An alligator was gliding along the otherwise quiet lake. No ducks today.

The gate was tied open with a wet and bloody tee shirt. There was a pool of blood on the concrete near the open gate and the grass leading down to the lake was crushed and bloody as if a bloody body had been dragged along, making a bloody-grass path into the water. The scream just came out of Peggy's throat involuntarily.

Five stories of lanais, all facing the lake, suddenly sprang to life as sleepy and outraged residents came out to see what was happening. One didn't disturb one's neighbors after all. That was against the rules.

"Can you please stop that caterwauling?" Gracie Anderson yelled down at Peggy "You'll wake the dead. Remember where you are. This isn't Coney Island."

"I'm screaming bloody murder," Peggy retorted as she stared at the pool of blood puddled near the open gate. "Nice dig about Coney Island, Gracie. Maybe you should tell it to the dead body in the lake."

Ever since Peggy had used the example of the Polar Bear Club going into the freezing waters of Coney Island, Gracie made it her business to snipe at the Brooklyn resort as if it was beneath her. Peggy knew she was doing it to be insulting but she had difficulty coming up with a nasty retort. Then too, she was hurt because she'd thought Gracie was her friend, and she loved Coney Island.

Peggy's logical mind was already going through the facts systematically. She loved logic and facts, above all else, and was intolerant of guessing games, made up facts and ridiculous theories. Seeing the puddle of blood on the pool deck, the gate tied open with a bloody tee shirt and the bloody grass path to the lake, Peggy surmised that this was, indeed, murder "most foul".

Her eyes travelled down the bloody path to the lake at the facedown body. And then, she watched in horror, as the meandering alligator slid into the lake, disappeared for a moment, then rose up from the murky waters and clasped its jaws on the body, and dragged it under the water, all in a moment's time.

Panicking, Peggy turned and was relieved to see the sheriff ambling up to the pool, a smirk on his face as he approached her, calling through the fence, "What's all this screaming about, Ma'am?" he said.

"That's what I'd like to know," Gracie Anderson yelled down from her lanai.

Sheriff Tate, hands on hips, gave a brief nod to Gracie who was shouting down from her fifth floor lanai, and he smiled condescendingly at Peggy. He glanced toward the lake and said, "What's all this about a body floating in the lake. I don't see it, but I did hear a lot of hollerin' as I walked up the path here."

Furious now, Peggy glared at the sheriff. She beckoned to the sheriff to follow her as she counted to ten, gritting her teeth. She led him to the secondary pool gate and pointed to the pool of blood underneath the gate. Then she pointed to the blood-laden grassy path leading down to the lake, and said in a low voice so Gracie, hanging over the railing of her lanai by now, wouldn't be able to hear what she said, "You missed the body, Sheriff. The alligator got her and pulled her down under the water as you strolled leisurely along the path, listening to my hollerin', as you so nicely put it."

He heard the anger and sarcasm in her voice and was horrified at the spectacle of blood she was pointing at. He pulled his cell phone out and called for help, advising those at the end of his call that he believes he has a possible murder on his hands, as well as a possible alligator attack. He turned on Peggy and, wanting to defend himself from this accusing woman, said, "I came as quickly as I could, ma'am.

"And you came with an attitude," Peggy answered him firmly.

"What's going on down there, sheriff," Gracie called down. "Don't let that woman bully you. She's a trouble-maker from New York, you know."

The sheriff took a long look at Peggy, who was obviously steaming mad at this point, and he wanted to calm the situation down. It was obvious to him that there was a problem with these two ladies. Maybe one of them was even the murderer.

"We have a problem, Ma'am," he called up to Gracie. "I'll be talking to you soon. You'll just have to be patient."

Other residents began calling down from their lanais. Sheriff Tate told them the whole pool and lake area was a crime scene and he was shutting the place down. No one was to come to these areas, he said. He had called for backup and for the forensics team.

The police arrived shortly after, and in the nick of time, because Roger West was leading an angry parade of Original Owners down to the pool area to "assert their rights". Roger wasn't one to take kindly to authorities infringing on his rights.

"I don't see why they had to close the pool," Roger complained loudly to his cohorts. He was the leader of the Original Owners, having been an original buyer in the Sea Grass complex. He spoke up at every meeting of the Association, and made complaints about everything and anything. He rarely used the pool but he was going to assert his rights to use it against the crime scene tape.

"This calls for an immediate Board meeting. I'm going to run for President this year and there won't be any unscheduled pool closings on my watch. I'm going to write to that worthless management company and register a formal complaint." He stamped his flip-flopped foot down for emphasis as his buddies nodded in agreement.

"What's this tape for," he groused, waving his long, spindly arms at the police tape dressing the chain link fence around the pool. As he made for the tape with his cane, a young police officer stepped out of the doorway to the clubhouse and said, "Sir, can I help you with anything?"

"Yes, sonny, you can take this tape away because I'm going in the pool." He sniped at the officer.

"Sorry, sir. This whole area is closed and you cannot go in there," the officer tried to explain, but Roger cut him off. "I'm an Owner here, young man, and I'll go wherever I please."

"This is a crime scene, sir, and you cannot enter the areas marked with the yellow tape," the officer replied politely.

Roger snarled at the young officer, who appeared to be losing his patience. As Roger waved his right arm in a dismissive gesture, the officer took his handcuffs out of his pocket and started to walk toward the Original Owners. They disbursed immediately and the officer put the cuffs away. "Okay, Gramps", he smiled, thinking of his own grandfather.

As he walked slowly away, Roger tried to assert his authority once more. "I see I can't even go fishing on the lake. You've got that stupid tape across the dock." He shook his head as if he couldn't believe the injustice being visited upon him. "I wanted a fish for dinner."

Sam Jefferson, his best friend, slapped him on the back as they retreated up the path to their building. "No, Roger, you won't be having fish tonight. Anyway, does anyone know what's going on? Why do we have a crime scene?"

Peggy Murray had been watching Roger and his friends, hoping they wouldn't get arrested. Roger was known to raise his cane when he was perturbed and she was afraid he'd push his luck with the police. She overheard Sam's question.

"Someone murdered Jenna Rivers," she said bluntly. "It was done at the pool and her body was dragged into the lake. Then an alligator got the body. That's why we are a crime scene, Sam."

Peggy walked away from the two Original Owners and rode the elevator up to the fourth floor. She had her belongings tucked neatly into her beach bag and she opened the door to her unit. "Are you back, Jack," she called as she put her keys on the console table in her hallway.

He answered from the den. "I'm back. Shot a lousy game, but it was fun. What's going on here?" he said, coming out into the hallway.

"Someone killed Jenna Rivers at the pool and dragged her body into the lake. An alligator made off with her body right before the sheriff got here. I'm the one who saw her in the lake and called the police. And," she said in her best sarcastic voice, which was tending to reach high soprano levels, "I'm never speaking to Gracie Anderson again!"

Jack, her husband of thirty-eight years, walked over and put his hands on her shoulders. "Come and sit down, Peg," he said. "You've had a bad time of it. You found the body?"

"I saw her in the lake. Then, when I tried to see if she needed help, I found the pool of blood and saw the grassy path where she was dragged into the lake. I called the police and I guess I screamed. Gracie has been mocking me all morning and the sheriff was snarky to me. Now the whole place is a crime scene. Maybe we should go back to Brooklyn. I'm never speaking to Gracie Anderson again," Peggy said, on the verge of tears.

"I'll make some coffee," Jack said. "Try to relax. You've had a terrible morning. I'm sorry I wasn't here for you. But, you'll be happy to know, Herb Anderson told me they're going back to Boston, so you won't be putting up with her for very long. He played a lousy game this morning and then told us they didn't want to be here anymore. They're putting their unit on the market and heading back to Massachusetts as soon as they can pack."

"But", Peggy said, "They're not from Boston. Gracie told me they're from Illinois. So, why did he say they're going back to Boston?"

"You know I didn't even realize that until you just said it. They both said they were from Illinois."

"Something's rotten in Denmark," Peggy murmured, almost to herself.

"What's with Hamlet, Peg?" Jack said, laughing. "Do you realize you've been quoting Hamlet for days?"

"Don't be silly, Jack, "she said, then laughed. "I guess I have been. It must be the chilly air. That play always made me feel chilly. But really, why would he say they're going back to Boston when they never said they were from Boston? And why," she continued, "would they be leaving here in such a rush?

"Really," Peggy continued. "I can't believe it. I wonder what brought this on. She always said how glad she was to get away from Chicago and all that lake snow in the winter. Now they're running to Boston in the early spring? They just got here. Why did they even come down at all? I wonder what's really going on."

They walked out to their lanai and Jack brought the coffee pot back from the kitchen where it had been washed and plugged it in, while Peggy brought the cream and sugar.

"All I know," Jack began as he poured their coffee, "is that he got a call on his cell. It had to be Gracie. They have a signal. She rings once, hangs up and rings again. That way he takes it out of his pocket and answers it. He spoke for a minute, hung up and his game went to pieces after that. When we finished playing he blurted out that they were leaving, putting their place on the market, and going back to Boston for good. Then he was quiet all the way home. Never said another word.

"It's only a five minute drive from the golf course to Sea Grass, so it wasn't an interminable amount of time for an awkward silence." Jack said and shook his head. "It really is strange, but I don't want you to get involved."

Peggy shook her head in disbelief. "I really don't want any part of any of this."

Jack continued to talk. "If the alligator got the body, how do you know it was Jenna Rivers?" he asked.

"They found her body in the reeds on the other side of the lake by the old fishing pier. Evidently the alligator left it there for a later snack. At least that's what the sheriff said. Anyway, it was Jenna, in a red pantsuit.

"I never saw her out so early. And not even dressed for swimming. Never saw her in the pool either. I just can't believe this is happening here. I seem to be rambling. The answer is I saw her in that red pantsuit earlier yesterday and again last night. Actually, I thought it odd that she hadn't changed for the big dinner."

She stood up and spoke loud enough for the neighbors to hear her, knowing most of them were out on their lanais watching the police down by the pool. She raised an eyebrow so Jack would understand what she was about. She was informing the Lanai Telegraph Line.

"And now, on top of a weird murder, the Andersons suddenly decide to leave Sea Grass immediately? That's very strange. The police told us all we were to be interviewed. I wonder what they'll say if the Andersons suddenly pick up stakes and rush off to Boston."

Jack smiled at her. He knew Peggy was just getting started on sorting out whatever facts were accumulating about this incident. She had solved several small crimes back home in Brooklyn, but never anything as awful as murder. "I think you might have a point there," he said and smiled, conspiratorially.

Within five minutes of their conversation on the lanai, they heard a loud knocking on their door.

They looked at each other and laughed. Simultaneously they said, "The Andersons are here."

Chapter Five:
Meet the Andersons

"So, why the sudden move back to Boston?" Peggy blurted out as soon as she opened the door to the Anderson's knock, with extra emphasis on the "back to Boston".

"Can you ask us in before grilling us first?" Gracie retorted. "And try to keep your voice down, Peggy. The lanais have ears," Gracie said, obviously aware that Peggy had already sent the message that the Andersons were leaving on the "lanai telegraph network", and, that the implication was, under suspicious circumstances.

Jack stepped aside and showed the Andersons into the living room. Everyone sat down.

"Aren't you going to offer us a drink or something?" Gracie exclaimed, her lacquered blond curls bobbing in time with her speech.

"For the love of Mike!" Herb whispered. "Can you stop bickering for a minute, Gracie? We didn't come for a drink. If they don't want to offer us hospitality, that's alright with me."

Jack stood up. "What'll you have?" he said, genially, a very amused smile playing loosely around his mouth.

"I'll have a gin and tonic," Herb said immediately. "Gracie will have her usual, white wine spritzer." He added.

Peggy sat and stared at what she considered a bizarre visit from the Andersons, and she couldn't help but say, "Are you both mad? You announce that you're leaving immediately, that you put your place on the market already, and you stop in here demanding hospitality with a murderer on the loose in this complex. What is going on with you two?" she demanded. "How are you going back to Boston when you told us you were from Chicago?"

Jack handed the Andersons their drinks and went into the kitchen to find some snacks, which he knew would be the next request. He returned with potato chips and peanuts in two bowls.

Herb Anderson stood up, drink in hand. "We've been offered a great opportunity in Boston. We're hurrying back to sell our place in Chicago. Spring is real estate season and we don't want to lose it. We're leaving tonight."

Jack put the snacks on the coffee table and said, "Alright. You can put your place on the market from here with one phone call. What is really going on? Why the rush? I'll bet the police will be asking you the same questions.

"This was in the door when I came home from our golf date," Jack continued. "It's a memo from the police informing us we should all be at the clubhouse tomorrow morning for an association meeting that the police will attend. I'm sure you got one too. So what will we tell them happened to the Andersons?" Peggy's raised eyebrows indicated that he hadn't told her of the notice in the door.

Herb stood up. "Tell them whatever you want. It's no skin off my nose. My rich uncle Bill died last night and we were just informed that we have inherited his estate in Back Bay. If we ever leave Boston, we won't be coming back here. So," he raised his glass in a mock toast to his host, "here's good bye to you guys. It's been nice knowing you for the most part, but we are happy to say, bye, ta ta, and adieu." With that the two Andersons stood up, put their empty glasses on the glass coffee table in the Murray's white living room, and walked out of the Murray's condo.

Jack and Peggy looked at each other, shrugged their shoulders and laughed. Jack walked across the room to close the door the Andersons left open on their way out.

"So nice of them to say goodbye. Guess we were really good friends and didn't know it," Jack said. He shook his head. "That was really so strange that I'm going to forget about it. Let's go have our coffee on the lanai."

As Peggy gathered her thoughts, another knock came to their door. "Are they back?" she wondered aloud as Jack went to open the door.

"You don't think," she began but checked her thought as she watched Jack swing the door open wide.

It was a stranger. She showed them a badge in a leather wallet and introduced herself. "I'm detective de Leon. May I come in? I'd like to ask Mrs. Murray a few questions, if that's alright."

She was a tall and athletically built woman in her early fifties. She had dark hair and clear blue eyes and very regular features. She reminded Peggy of one of the officers on one of the police television shows from years ago. Cagney and Lacie, I think. She looks like Lacie, she decided.

"Why don't you join us on the lanai," Jack said. "We were having some coffee and you're welcome to have a cup with us."

The three of them walked through the living room and out onto the lanai where Jack had left the coffee maker plugged in. Peggy brought out an extra coffee mug, which she filled for the detective.

"What can I do for you, Detective," she asked.

"I just want you to write down the events as you found them this morning, while it's still fresh in your mind," she said as she opened her attaché case and put a pad of lined paper and a pen on the table. "I really hate to bother you but it's important that you do this before time passes or other people distract you with their opinions."

"Of course," Peggy replied. "It's still very fresh in my mind and I haven't really spoken to anyone about it. Just to Sheriff Tate and a few words to my nosey neighbor, Gracie Anderson. You don't have to worry about her, though, since she's leaving for Boston, I think immediately. Isn't that the impression you got too, Jack," she added, picking up the pad and the pen.

Detective de Leon stood up. "Who are the Andersons and which is their unit?" she said, taking out her phone.

"They're in 502," Jack said. "They just left here. They seemed to be in quite a rush. Maybe you can catch them if you hurry."

"Ill be back for your statement," Detective de Leon said as she headed to the door, speaking to someone on her cell phone.

She was back within the hour. Apologizing for the intrusions, she asked Peggy if she had completed her statement.

"Yes, of course I did," she said, handing her back her pad and pen, having written a two-page statement. "Did you find the Andersons?" she asked.

"Thank you ma'am," was the only answer Detective de Leon gave her. "I'll be seeing you and all your neighbors at the clubhouse tomorrow morning at ten o'clock. I'll be providing everyone who lives here with a few questions on a handout." With that she went to the door and let herself out.

"What do you think," Peggy asked Jack. "Did she catch up with the Andersons and are we all required to meet her at the Association meeting?"

"I really don't know, my dear, "Jack answered. "I wasn't even going to go to the meeting. I hate meetings, you know that."

"Well, Jack, as an officer, I have to go, and I'd really appreciate your support. I'm afraid I'll be put to the test tomorrow, especially if the Andersons come. They'll know we were trying to insinuate that they had a suspicious reason for rushing back to Boston. Rich uncle dying, indeed." Peggy finished.

Chapter Six:
The Association Meeting

The next morning came bright and warm. Peggy drank her morning coffee.

I wish Jack would come with me, she thought. She always felt like he grounded her.

Jack strolled leisurely into the kitchen and poured himself a mug of coffee.

"You have to come to the meeting, Jack. I really need your support." Peggy said imploringly. "You heard Detective de Leon. I have to be prepared to notice if anyone tries to give a false report of the happenings in the morning. You were right there when she told me I had to help her at the meeting." He smiled and shook his head, no.

"Okay, Jack," Peggy called to him as he picked up his golf bag and headed for the front door. "There'll come a time when you'll want me to do something for you and I'll just go and take my morning swim instead."

"I'll be sure to ask you in the afternoon," he laughed as he picked up his golf bag, gave her a quick peck on the cheek and ambled out the door.

And now she was alone. He had gone to play golf and she was mad at him. Why would Detective de Leon clear him from the meeting where she thought she was going to interrogate everyone, she wondered.

Peggy sat down at the desk in the living room. She'd had a good time furnishing the condo. She finally had an all white living room, but she knew it wouldn't remain white when the grandchildren came to visit. It's my own fault, she thought. Maybe I'll get some of those stretchy slipcovers they sell in that shoppers' mart down on Manatee Avenue. Aware that she was stalling, Peggy knew it was time to go to the meeting.

Resigned to being on her own, Peggy took out her notebook and looked over the copy of the statement she'd given to Detective de Leon. She'd had the presence of mind to photocopy the statement before giving it to the detective. She was always happy to have her well-stocked home office. She was going to take up writing some day.

What is it about Jenna Rivers that I'm missing here? She thought.

It was a short walk to the clubhouse from the elevator. Peggy rode down, apprehensive about the meeting. She didn't want to deal with her neighbors, especially the Andersons

Finally, notebook in hand, she headed to the clubhouse door.   From the look of things, she thought as she stared into the large windows on either side of the door, the place is packed. Here I thought people would be trying to avoid the meeting and it's packed.

Sure enough, Mabel Milano was in the front row surrounded by the gossip posse. It looked like Gracie Anderson had given her back leadership of the posse. Gracie was not sitting with "the crew", as the committee organizers regularly called themselves.

Peggy walked to the front of the room and took her place at the long table which served as the dais, erected in front of the rows of chairs placed audience-style for the meeting. The other tables were pushed against the wall.

Peggy sat, her notebook on the table in front of her. She had to hide her aversion to Mable Milano. Mable was an ignorant loud mouth, according to Peggy. She constantly made her opinions known, whether or not you were interested, and God help the person who would either question her opinions or disagree with them. They went into her gossip bin and were tossed like a spinach salad. Wherever and whenever Mable got the chance to bring up their disagreement, it was a done deal.

She reminded Peggy of a classmate she had in high school. No one was safe from Doris' sharp tongue. It was so bad, people backed out of a room they were entering if they saw Doris there. Maybe she was just picking on Mable.

Peggy came out of her reverie when Ralph Winston walked into the clubhouse.

He was a tall man in his late sixties. Tall and urbane, Ralph was a retired New York City policeman. His silver hair was full and his dark eyes sparkled like diamond cut black onyx. He was a tennis champion.

President Ralph Winston walked to the center of the table and called the meeting to order. He asked Peggy to read the minutes of the last meeting. As she stood to read the minutes, she noticed the Andersons slipping into the back row alongside Detective de Leon.

The minutes were accepted and Ralph turned the meeting over to new business.

Roger West leaped to his feet before anyone had a chance to say another word. Peggy saw Detective de Leon take her cell phone out and speak into it. Moments later, at least half dozen uniformed police officers entered the room. As they started to take up positions around the room, Roger rushed toward the double doors that led to the pool, shaking off his robe as he ran. They all watched through the glass wall separating the pool from the social room as he jumped into the pool before anyone could stop him, with two officers in pursuit.

Everyone held their breath as they heard him scream and then, they heard several shots blasting the air.

Mabel screamed, "They shot poor Roger!"

"They did not," Peggy yelled at her. "He screamed before the shots were heard."

"You're a regular detective, aren't you?" smirked Mable.

"Yes, I am," Peggy answered for want of something else to say. She really wasn't too quick with nasty retorts.

Detective de Leon took Ralph's place at the front of the room and shushed the gathering.

"The alligator was in the pool, people, and had to be shot. Mr. West is being arrested for his little game and we are calling the authorities to come for the alligator's carcass. The pool is closed until the health department clears it. Now, no one is to pull any more stunts, or you will be arrested. You may proceed with your meeting. I will be handing out forms for you to fill in so that I can arrange interviews with those who might have information. Some interviews will take a few minutes, and others will be longer. It depends. I'll hand out the forms after your meeting." She finished and sat down.

Ralph Winston walked to the center of the room. "We can now continue with new business." He said calmly.

Mabel Milano walked to the front of the room and practically overpowered the podium. She had a sheaf of papers in her hand which she held up as though it were an exhibit in a trial. She had a very angry expression on her face.

"Now what's the matter, Mabel," someone called out from the audience. "You're looking quite perturbed for a change," Sam Matthews practically cackled at her. He was one of the Original Owners.

Mabel glared at him. "The matter is Claudia Robbins," she snarled at him through clenched teeth. "Or, "she continued, "Just Plain Claudia, as she insists on calling herself. She has become a danger, not only to herself but to all of us.

"She continues to tie the gates of the pool open, because, she says, we shouldn't deny anyone entrance to the pool in this hot climate. I don't think we agree with her, and now this! She probably let that alligator into the pool and it killed poor Jenna! And, she's responsible for the alligator that nearly got poor Roger. I, for one, want her out of here!" Mable fairly screamed as she walked to her seat, dabbing her eyes as she went.

The door to the clubhouse slammed open. Everyone jumped at the noise. Claudia, or Claudia Robbins as she was formerly known back in the days when she used her last name, stormed into the room.

"I heard every word you said, Mabel Milano, Milano, Milano," she sneered as she took over the podium. "I was listening outside and you have a big mouth. I will open those gates to the poor souls who don't have a pool, whether you, and your boring board like it or not. So there! You have it, you mean-spirited witch. You're just a bigoted snob." Claudia laughed as loud as she could and took a seat in the front row, right next to Mabel.

Bessie Matthews walked directly to the podium. "I just want to say that I second everything Mabel just said. I am in total agreement with her." Bessie smiled at the assemblage, nodded at Claudia, and walked away.

Kathryn Sands strolled up to the podium. Mrs. Jerry Sands was a very poised, tall, stunning former model. "I am here to agree that the matter before us is the flagrant breaking of the rules by Ms. Claudia. Tying that gate open is an invitation to the alligators that we all know she feeds. I have it on my camera, Claudia feeding the alligators. I am sending the clip to the police. She needs to go to jail."

It was as though someone had stirred a pot of boiling stew. Everyone started yelling and putting in his or her opinions. Finally Ralph made it to the podium and called for order.

"We can't have this," he said, calmly, using the microphone. "Miss Claudia," he said, almost quietly, "You cannot tie the gates to the pool open. You cannot invite non-members into the pool. There are public pools for everyone to use. Indeed, county pools where anyone can get a pass. Our pool is not large enough to open to the public, nor are we insured for that. We don't have a lifeguard and a child could wander into the pool and be harmed with that gate open."

"You mean you just don't want poor people in the pool," she screeched. "I'll open the pool to all. Animals need to eat and people need to cool off."

"She's crazy," Mabel shouted, still dabbing her eyes. "She might as well have killed poor Jenna."

Claudia shouted at her. "You're just a bigoted snob, Mabel Milano. Everyone has a right to cool off in this heat."

With that said, Miss Claudia pushed Mabel off her chair!

The members all gasped and one yelled out, "She needs to be kicked out of this complex!"

Peggy Murray suppressed what could have become a loud laughing fit.

"Order," shouted Ralph. "Miss Claudia," he continued, "That did it," Ralph shouted, "Harry, please escort Miss Claudia from the premises."

Claudia glared at him. "Ralph Roister Doister!" she snarled at him. It was her favorite taunt at the president, making fun of his name.

Obviously, Peggy thought, Miss Claudia has knowledge of sixteenth century comedy plays. I wonder if she has a degree in English literature.

Harry Rafferty, the Sergeant at Arms, struggled to his feet. He was a former football player who was nearing his eighty-seventh year. He grasped his cane and rose to his full height and started to walk toward the glowering Miss Claudia.

The room was suddenly quiet. Miss Claudia stood with her hands on her hips.

Everyone held his or her collective breath. More than one person wondered whether Miss Claudia would go quietly or would she attack poor old Harry. She was known, occasionally, to get physical.

"Miss Claudia," Harry began, "kindly accompany me to the door."

She sat there smirking at him. "And, if I don't," she said, laughing and rocking back and forth. "What will you do about it, old Harry?" she laughed. "Old goat, old chum, old stick!" she continued.

Ralph rushed to help Mabel who was struggling to her feet. She stood over Miss Claudia and clenched her fists. "If I weren't a lady I'd slap that silly grin off your nasty face, Miss Claudia!" she growled through clenched teeth.

Harry, red-faced at Claudia's insults, raised his cane but Jerry Sands stopped him.

"She's crazy, Harry. Don't bother with her. The police will escort her out."

Peggy opened her eyes wide. Jerry looks rumpled and wrinkled. He's usually so well groomed that he looks like what my mother would call a collar ad. No tie, five o'clock shadow at nine in the morning?

Detective de Leon and two officers walked up and put the cuffs on Miss Claudia. The officers walked her out the door.

Sheriff Tate entered the clubhouse and said, "I see Miss Claudia is going back to the hospital. What a surprise."

Kathryn Sands, still at the podium, said, "May I continue?"

Ralph said, "Of course, Kathryn. Please continue."

"The management must do something about her. She is a danger to us all and I for one have had enough of her."

"We are trying, Kathryn, but it is her only domicile and you know how hard it is to evict someone from their only home in Florida." Ralph said.

Kathryn rose up to her full height. "Then get those stupid doctors to have her committed. She just has to be out of here." Kathryn stormed off to her seat. It was obvious that Kathryn was upset about something other than Miss Claudia. She was not sitting with her husband either.

Mabel Milano walked to the podium. "I am going to press charges against her for knocking me down. Maybe that will rid us of her. I want a vote taken to expel her from this complex. My grandchildren will be here next week and I don't want them attacked in the pool. I'm sure she murdered Jenna." Mabel stomped to her seat and folded her arms across her chest.

Peggy shook her head and murmured more to herself than to anyone, "I don't think so."

Chapter Seven: The Association Meeting Continues

Bessie Matthews walked to the podium.

"I don't want to start any more trouble than we already have, but, I feel I must put in a word of support for my friend, Mabel Milano, who was so rudely treated by Miss Claudia…"

The door slammed open and Miss Claudia burst into the room as if she was a Broadway star looking for her due, her moment of raucous applause.

"How…?" someone called out.

"I have friends," Claudia shouted, bowing and smiling to the assembly. Then she turned her attention to Bessie Matthews.

"Really, Bessie Matthews. You should not talk about rudeness and manners." She cackled. "Not with that husband of yours. How about when he shaved his head out by the air conditioner condensers! That was a pretty sight and, I'm sure, the best of manners. We all loved having his hair all over the flowers and plants. How could a lady such as you be married to such an oaf! I'm sure that was a violation of the rules." Her laugh could have broken a few windows.

Bessie was enraged. "How dare you, you rank lowlife. I'll have you know that I also took a video of you feeding the alligators in the lake, which is against the law. I'm going to send it to the authorities. I have no intention of facing an alligator either in the pool or on the pool deck. I have a picture of you tying that gate open."

Claudia stood up menacing Bessie. "I doubt even an alligator would be interested in you," she sneered.

Peggy jotted down a note to herself. Did Bessie's photo of Claudia tying the gate open show Jerry and Jenna dancing last night?

"That will be enough," Ralph said. "Any other new business?" he asked, wearily.

Bessie glared at him. "It's not enough!" She held up her i-pad. "Here's a video of Miss Claudia just last night feeding the alligator off the dock." The video showed Miss Claudia holding up pieces of raw chicken and tossing them into the lake. Then it plainly showed Miss Claudia walking back to the pool gate and tying it open with a white cloth. There was no blood on the white cloth. A gasp went up from the assembly.

Detective de Leon sat up straight. You could hear the music from the clubhouse and, barely visible, a shadowy couple could be seen dancing on the pool deck.

"And just this morning, according to the news, a woman was found, not two miles from here, with an alligator in her pool, where he broke into the lanai right through the screen." Bessie finished and sat down emphatically.

Claudia cackled and screamed, "They gotta eat too!"

"That will be quite enough, Claudia," Ralph said taking over the podium. "Sit down and be quiet or I'll have you taken out again. I mean it. Any other new business before I turn the meeting over to Detective de Leon?"

Bessie stood her ground. "Claudia tied that gate open late last night and that's where Jenna was killed." She ended triumphantly.

Vince Morgan stood up. "I just want to inform all of you that I am representing Miss Claudia from here on in, and I don't want to have to warn any of you a second time about spreading dangerous rumors about her. That's all," he finished and sat down.

"You're just getting into this because you're jealous of Jerry Sands' law practice and you're retired," Mable shouted. "Why do you have to save her from being put where she belongs!"

Claudia stood up, hands on hips. She tossed her hair, and after a dramatic pause, she glared at the crowd. "Look to Jerry Sands. I think he did it. He was seen running around the mall with Jenna Rivers. I have it on good authority. And," she added, cackling, "he was seen dancing with her on the pool deck late last night, dancing cheek to cheek. I saw them myself! Right after I tied the gate open, but the tee shirt wasn't bloody yet." She sat down and crossed her arms, a triumphant toss of her head and she was silent.

Kathryn Sands stood up, glanced around the room, picked up her enormous tote bag and strode out of the clubhouse.

Peggy Murray frowned. That's the way she left last night, she thought. She knew Jerry was with Jenna.

Again, Vince Morgan stood up, but this time he walked to the podium and faced the group. "I am warning everyone once more, be very careful about throwing around accusations and innuendoes."

His silver hair, shining in the sunshine that was piercing through the wall of windows, gave him a look of extreme dignity as he walked back to his seat, Hawaiian shirt replacing what would have been his dark suit in his active days.

Peggy shook her head. Maybe retirement isn't the right goal, she thought. He's a shadow of what he must have been. It's so weird. But he still has a professional air and he's right to defend poor Claudia. Still, she needs help.

Ralph nodded at the retired attorney and said, "Detective de Leon will now address you regarding the recent tragedy. I would ask everyone to be attentive and, perhaps, we can even be of help to the investigation."

Detective de Leon walked to the podium.

" I need your help," she addressed the assemblage of residents. "Does anyone know the deceased's husband, or if she has any family?"

A tall, well-dressed brunette rose to her feet.

"I'm Barbara Rivers-Smyth." She said. "The victim's husband is my father."

"Thank you, Mrs. Smyth", the detective said. "I would like to interview you privately, after this meeting." She motioned to a uniformed policewoman who approached Mrs. Smyth, clipboard in hand.

She continued addressing the association. "In order to stop all the speculation I've heard this morning, I will tell you, Mrs. Rivers died of a gun shot wound."

Another uniformed officer began handing out stapled packets to the assembly.

"You are now receiving handouts with directions. I would ask you to look over the materials and if you have any information please fill it out, hand it to one of the officers, or your recording secretary, and we will make an appointment to interview you."

"Why does Peggy Murray get to collect the handouts?" whined Mabel Milano.

Her comment was ignored by everyone.

Detective de Leon continued. "Mrs. Rivers had been drugged prior to being shot. I have asked your recording secretary and Officer Davis to collect the handouts when you finish with them. If you have additional information that you think might bear on this incident, there's room at the bottom of page two. For example, if you saw anyone on the pool deck between ten o'clock and two this morning, or if you heard anything at all, I would appreciate whatever information you may have. I will be making appointments to interview some of you. Mr. Sands, you will please come with me."

Detective de Leon walked out of the clubhouse, gathering the Andersons with her as she left.

Peggy looked around, nonplussed. She picked up her notebook and waited to see if anyone was going to approach her with his or her filled-out forms. She looked at her own handout. There was a place for her name, unit number and a telephone number. The date of the incident and a "time span" followed by five lines to print in where she was on that date and in that time span. She filled it in and added her comments about when and where she'd last seen the victim. She was dancing with Jerry Sands, as Miss Claudia said. I'll bet I wasn't the only one who saw Jerry Sands with her last night. It's on the video.

That was a weird thing for that detective to say, she thought. Why does she need me to help Officer Davis collect forms? And she seems to be hanging onto or with the Andersons. Maybe they're suspects, she laughed to herself.

Jenna was drugged? I saw Jerry Sands spilling something from an envelope into her drink. I saw them dancing on the pool deck in the moonlight last night. I saw a pool of blood and a bloody matted grass path to the lake this morning. When was she killed? I saw her with Jerry sometime after one or two in the morning. I'll have to ask Jack what time I came home. I had such a headache last night, which seems to be about to erupt again today.,

Peggy looked around. No customers. I'm going home and take an aspirin and a long nap, she thought.

Maybe I should run down to the store and get something in for dinner, she thought. Then I can take it easy for the rest of the day.

As she walked back to her building, Detective de Leon caught up with her.

"Did anyone come by and give you any information, Mrs. Murray?"

"Not one person," Peggy replied. "I was quite surprised but maybe no one wants to get involved. I certainly don't. Good luck, Detective."

Detective de Leon looked down at Peggy's filled in handout. "I will need to interview you this afternoon around four" she said and left quickly. "I'll meet you in the clubhouse. I've made arrangements to have it for interviews."

This was a particularly annoying day, Peggy thought, driving back from the store. She bought a large, frozen lobster mac and cheese for dinner and was looking forward to lying down and watching some harmless television. No news tonight.

She was pulling into her parking spot. That new neighbor had parked her car over the line again, and partially into Peggy's spot. This is so irritating, she thought. I really do miss my garage. Condo living is very annoying when your neighbors can't seem to know their place. That fool should learn how to park. I ought to find out who my parking neighbor is and tell him or her off.

No I don't think that would be a good idea. I'm really unsettled again. Why don't I get myself organized and rethink what it is that's really going on here.

Why do I even care what's going on here, she thought, angrily taking her purchases in her canvas-lined grocery cart and heading for the elevator. Oh, no, she thought, seeing Mabel Milano holding the elevator for her. "I'm just dropping in on Gracie," Mabel said. "I really want to hear what she thinks about our murder here. Are you going to see Gracie too?"

"No," Peggy answered wearily. "I'm heading for a nice long shower, a light supper, and a night of watching television."

She didn't bother to tell Mabel that Gracie wouldn't be home. She didn't tell Mabel that she was being interviewed at four o'clock. She had one hour to take an aspirin and a cold glass of water before heading, once again, to the clubhouse.

Peggy put her food away and headed for her desk. She started one of her famous lists.

"What time did Peggy die? Where was Jerry? How did the tee shirt I saw Claudia carry out to the deck get bloody? Why did Jerry Sands drug Jenna? Would he drug her and then shoot her? That can't be right. What does Jerry know? I think he's a warthog but not a killer. "

I'd like to talk to Jenna's husband's daughter. She must know something about her father's wife even if she didn't like her. Where did she meet her father? Where is she from? We really don't know anything about her except she had a lot of money to spend on herself.

Peggy walked over to her laptop and searched the name Jenna Rivers. Many names popped up, some even in the right age and location bracket, but none of them were this Jenna. Their brief bios did not match Jenna Rivers of Sea Grass Condominium Complex.

She needed more information.

It was five minutes before four o'clock. Peggy left a note for Jack and left for her interview. She reached the clubhouse at exactly four o'clock.

Much to her surprise, Detective de Leon was not alone in the clubhouse. There, sitting at the table with the detective, were Mr. and Mrs. Jerry Sands and Miss Claudia. Kathryn Sand's phone was on the table.

"I'm glad you could make it, Mrs. Murray," the detective said. "I see on your form that you not only saw Mr. Sands and Mrs. Rivers dancing on the pool deck late that night, but before that, in the clubhouse, you said you saw Mr. Sands putting something in Mrs. Rivers' drink. Please elaborate on that incident, Mrs. Murray," the detective finished.

Peggy folded her hands on the table in front of her. "I saw Jerry Sands spill an envelope of some substance into a glass of wine, I presume it was wine. Some time after that, I left the party, and when I walked through the pool area, I saw Jerry Sands and Jenna Rivers dancing on the pool deck. I saw Miss Claudia ahead of me as I walked to the elevator in the Manatee building. Miss Claudia reached the elevator before I did and I had to wait for it to come back down. I thought I heard something but then, I thought it was nothing. Looking back, I think it might have been a shot, but I can't be sure. That's all I remember except it was sometime after two in the morning when I finally got home."

Claudia looked up and said in a quiet voice, "I would have held the elevator for you, Peggy, had I seen you."

Peggy nodded to her. "I know you would have, Claudia."

Jerry Sands looked awful. He cleared his throat. "I did put a drug into Jenna's wine. I couldn't get anywhere with her and I wondered what her game was. Please, I'm sorry. I cannot lose my legal license. I'm losing my wife and I have to be able to support myself. I didn't kill her." He was crying.

Kathryn Sands sat stonily silent. Finally she spoke. "He arrived at our condo a little after two in the morning. He looked like a mess, blood on his hands, crying for my help, the fool.

"He told me they were dancing and she suddenly went limp in his arms, and he felt her warm blood on his hands. He then walked her over toward the gate. She wasn't dead yet. She grasped at the tee shirt holding the gate open. Our hero here," she said, glaring at her husband, "then, he apparently left this dying woman, clutching at the tee shirt and the gate, and fled home to me. I let him wait out the night on my lanai, but he cannot come back to my property except to finish getting his personal belongings out. That's all I have to say, except I didn't know he'd left her there to die until this morning."

They were all dismissed by the detective, with a warning to Jerry Sands, "Mr. Sands, you might be charged for the drugging incident. The District Attorney will decide, not me."

Peggy left the clubhouse. What a mess, she was thinking. How can people get themselves into such stupid messes? Jerry's a fool, but he's not a killer. What a wimp. He knew she was mortally wounded and he ran for cover. I hope for Kathryn's sake the D.A. doesn't prosecute him for the date rape drug. She really doesn't need to deal with that mess and she'd be dragged into it.

Chapter Eight: It's Friendship

It was a beautiful morning and Barbara Rivers Smyth took a deep breath and felt at peace with herself for the first time since she'd come to Bradenton. She was getting things done, cleaning up the mess she'd found here. She thought it was unusual to have the buildings named for Florida aquatic animals. Her father was in The Manatee.

Barbara walked up to the second floor of the building named The Dolphin, and approached the unit where she'd followed Jenna that fateful day. As soon as she heard that Kathryn Sands had put her husband out of her condo because of Jenna Rivers, she'd felt responsible for their breakup. She didn't know the rest of the story. He swore it was a professional relationship but Kathryn didn't buy that. Yet, Barbara could attest that Jerry Sands was doing legal work for Jenna and felt it was her duty to tell his wife.

Barbara arranged for a care-giver service to come every morning to take care of her father when she discovered that the care-giver Jenna had arranged for her father was a mélange of good-natured neighbors she'd imposed upon. Pleased with the woman the service provided, Barbara took advantage of the help and decided to visit Kathryn Sands and apologize for creating the ruckus that led to the breakup of her marriage. She also met the next-door neighbor who brought a casserole over as soon as she'd moved in. Barbara was so grateful that this woman was caring for her father since Jenna's death.

Kathryn opened the door and looked at Barbara with surprise.

She recognized Barbara as the woman who exposed Jerry and Jenna for what they were, but she didn't know why she had been following Jenna or why she was so angry with her. Then she remembered, this is the woman who had identified herself as Jenna's husband's daughter. Jenna, on the other hand, was just one of Jerry's silly women in Kathryn's eyes.

"Yes," she queried. "What can I do for you?"

"My name is Barbara Rivers Smyth. I'm Walter Rivers' daughter. I've come to apologize for my behavior the other day. I know I've caused you serious trouble and I'm sorry. I had no right to involve you by creating that scene. I'm really very sorry. I didn't mean to cause trouble between you and your husband."

"Come in, please," Kathryn said, and showed Barbara inside her apartment.

When they were comfortably seated, on her beautiful lanai, Kathryn said, "You are not responsible for the breakup of this marriage. I never should have married him. He's a divorce lawyer and he takes a new mistress with each new client. He only represents women. I was a widow and I think he came after me because he knew I was well fixed.

"This condo is only one of my properties and he won't get a thing from me because I had a real lawyer write up my pre-nup agreement. I just decided I was finished with his nonsense. So, you don't have anything to feel guilty about. I knew he was meeting someone and all you did was show me who it was."

"Well, this is a situation," Barbara said. "I just wanted to tell you that your husband did some legal work for Jenna. She was trying to get legal control of all my father's assets. I just wanted you to know that was true."

She stood up. "I've taken up enough of your time. I'm going to see that woman who's on the board, a Mrs. Murray. I need to make my staying here legal. I was informed by the next-door neighbor, Veronica something, that I have to let the board know who I am and how long I'm staying. I just wanted to apologize for my histrionics the other day. Now I'm considered a suspect because of my loud and public disagreements with Jenna."

"You're so upset," Kathryn said. "Why don't I get you a cold drink and we can talk a little. You're not to blame for anything and I think you could use a friend here. You see, I'm also considered a suspect because of Jerry and his fling with Jenna."

Barbara smiled. "It seems witnesses to a few of my loud confrontations with Jenna have come forward to the police."

"And I'm the woman scorned," Kathryn quipped.

"Oh, look," Barbara said, looking down at the pool. "There's Mrs. Murray now. She seems like she's leaving the pool now so maybe I can catch up with her and ask her what I have to do. Your lanai feels like it's almost on the pool deck, you're so close."

"Yes," Kathryn answered. "I took this unit because it's on the corner and the building angles out that way. It feels like it's almost on the pool deck.

'I see Peggy Murray. You're right. She seems to be talking to Veronica. I think she's your new neighbor. Peggy is on the fourth floor of your building," Kathryn finished.

Barbara watched a moment as Peggy stood talking to a woman. "I guess that's the water aerobics class coming in. Veronica told me they're going to have water aerobics three days a week at eight-thirty starting next week."

Kathryn nodded. "I did hear about that. I might even join the class. I see that instructor is talking to Peggy. I heard Peggy's annoyed because she likes to swim every morning at eight and this will interfere with her routine. Evidently this is the last day the instructor can come in the afternoon."

"What is that other woman doing?" Barbara said, pointing to Mabel Milano who was carrying a boom box over to the side of the pool.

Kathryn laughed. "It looks like she's going to plug that old boom box into the outside plug. I guess they'll have music for their class. I hope I don't have to complain if the music gets too loud. Well, I really won't be able to complain if I join the class.

"I think Peggy Murray is discussing the schedule of the class. She doesn't like to have her routines disrupted, I hear. Her old friend, Gracie Anderson, evidently helped arrange this schedule to annoy Peggy. You wouldn't believe what goes on, sometimes. Otherwise it's a nice place to visit. I hope I haven't given you the wrong impression."

Barbara shook her head. "I would have thought that there should have been a discussion before the class was put in place. I'll try to see Mrs. Murray at a better time. I don't feel like running into any discussions right now. I really must get back to my father. The Care woman will be leaving soon." Barbara turned to leave.

Kathryn walked Barbara to the door. "I agree. I don't want to get into that either. I'm thinking about going back to North Dakota as soon as my divorce lawyer doesn't need me and I probably won't be back until next season, if at all."

"I'll be taking my father back to Georgia as soon as I can leave." Barbara said.

The two women looked at each other for a moment, and then they were distracted by Veronica, who appeared to be walking toward the aerobics instructor, her limp very pronounced.

"Do you think she's going to join the class?" Kathryn said.

"It might be good for her. She seems quite lame. Oh, well, I must be going. I've taken up enough of your time, Kathryn. I would say it was nice meeting you, except for the circumstances. We have so much in common," Barbara said as she began to walk out of the condo.

Kathryn answered, "If you have any trouble with the board, let me know. I own several of these condos and I think I have some pull with a few of the members. Here we are, two homicide suspects, thanks to Jenna. If it wasn't so awful it would be funny."

"I'm a suspect because I've been observed arguing with her. I did threaten to have her arrested if she did anything to my father." Barbara said, and smiled.

"Was she a wicked step-mother?" Kathryn said almost sarcastically.

"Never," Barbara said in horror at the thought. "She was a CNA in the nursing home where my father was living. She married him and took him here before I found out about it, so I came here to see what she was up to. He's very ill and I want to take him back home when I'm free to go."

"What a mess," Kathryn exclaimed. "It seems like we're both in a mess because of dear departed Jenna."

"I think," Barbara said, "there are more suspects who would have murdered her than just the two of us."

Kathryn nodded. "I think you are probably right. Let's just hope the police find out who it was so we can get on with our lives."

Chapter Nine: Who is Jenna Rivers?

I really need to stay out of this mess, Peggy thought as she straightened the cushions on the couch. But, something is bothering me about Barbara Rivers Smyth.

It was annoying that not one person came to her at the end of the meeting, now that she thought about it. She couldn't believe that no one wanted to, at least, gossip about what they thought were important details of the crime. And why did that detective make me look like I was some kind of sycophant. I'm not her assistant and I intend to stay out of this.

I need to know more about Jenna if I am to sort this out, just for myself, Peggy muttered to herself. I need to remember what it was that is nagging me.

There was knock on the door.

I hope that's not Mabel. I agreed to join the aerobics class so as not to make an issue of the timing of the class, or, that she and Gracie made all the arrangements without consulting the board. I'll just fold the class into my regular routine. Three days a week shouldn't kill me. I'll go down at seven so I can get my laps in before the class comes.

Peggy took her coffee mug with her and walked to the foyer and opened the door. There stood the woman who was crying that day at the Santervas Mall. She recognized her immediately, as someone she'd seen before. She is the one at the association meeting who said Jenna was her father's wife. That's what's been bothering me. She's the woman who was yelling and crying at Jenna at the mall.

"I know you don't know me," the woman began, "but I was at the meeting yesterday and I didn't want to come forward in front of everyone with all that ruckus going on. I know you're on the condominium board and I need some help. I want to move into my father's condo with him and I understand I need to apply and be approved by the Board."

Peggy nodded to her.

"I need to introduce myself," she said. "I am Barbara Rivers Smyth, Walter Rivers' daughter. Jenna had recently married my father and I came up here to see how he is and I ran into this mess."

"Of course," Peggy said as she opened the door wider and motioned Barbara inside. "How can I help you?"

Over coffee, Barbara related the whole tale of her father's unfortunate meeting up with Jenna Wagner and his subsequent marriage to her. Now she wanted to take him back to Georgia with her, close up the condo, and sell it. This murder was causing her to remain here, as the police believe she had a motive for killing Jenna, and there were some legal issues connected to disposing of the condo. Jenna's mother, Rosalie Wagner, had come out of the woodwork and was putting a claim on the condo.

Peggy was quiet. She was thinking about this poor woman's dilemma. Finally, she said, "Did Detective de Leon actually tell you that you're a suspect?"

Barbara breathed a deep sigh. "Not in so many words, exactly, but when I told her who I was she asked me, very pointedly, not to leave. I told her that when I heard about Jenna's death I moved out of my hotel and into my father's condo to take care of him, until I could take him back to Georgia."

"Why exactly would she think you would kill Jenna?" Peggy said, now clearly remembering the scene she'd witnessed at the mall.

"There were several scenes between Jenna and myself. There were witnesses, many of whom have already come forward and given statements."

"Really?" Peggy said as the scene she'd witnessed drifted into her memory.

"I just want to take my father home and get out of this place." The woman was overwrought. "I hated Jenna and everyone who knows me knows that."

Peggy looked at Barbara. "Sit down, won't you?" she offered. "What can you tell me about her, specifically. What did you hate about her?"

Barbara nodded. "Jenna was an opportunist. She was a CNA in the nursing home where my father was living. He had early onset Alzheimer's and the beginnings of Parkinson's. She was new there and one of the nurses called me because she was concerned about how attached my father was becoming to this new aide.

"I met her once but, unfortunately, I had no idea how fast she could operate. Before I knew it, they had married and they left Georgia right after the wedding.

"I hired a detective agency and he tracked them to Bradenton and this complex. Jenna barely cared for my father. I doubt if he's been out of that condo in months. She gives him breakfast and then he's alone all day, sometimes all night. Sometimes he was left without food. A neighbor told me she'd fed him before Jenna caught her and let her know she wasn't welcome.

"This is why I could be considered a suspect. I've had several open and loud confrontations with her, some witnessed by her boyfriend, that married lawyer. He was helping her take over my father's assets."

"Jerry Sands! She was with Jerry Sands!" exclaimed Peggy. "I remember seeing you arguing with her in the Santervas Mall. Actually, that was early the same day Jenna was murdered."

Barbara shook her head. "Yes, that was our last confrontation. Several people who witnessed that scene have already come forward. I didn't realize you were there too.

"On top of this, I had hired a good law firm to see if I could extricate my father from her clutches and take him home. But that also helps cast suspicion on me because, as my attorney advised me, it shows how far I would go to stop Jenna from benefiting from her marriage to my father." Barbara suddenly stopped talking.

"I guess I've really talked too much. I just need to make my staying with my father in this condo legal. I'm sorry I talked too much and took up so much of your time." She looked embarrassed.

"Why did Detective de Leon specifically say you were a suspect?" Peggy asked again.

"She told me she doesn't really regard me as a killer, but she must require me to stay here until I can be cleared. Since I really can't leave without creating a bigger problem, my lawyers have informed me, I might as well try to deal with my father's estate while I wait for some solution to Jenna's murder. So, I'm going to apply to be on my father's condo title and settle in for as long as I have to, or at least until I can clear my name. Then I'll take him home. I don't care who killed Jenna Wagner."

Peggy stood up, looked perplexed, but seeming to be lost in her own thoughts. Finally she shook her head. "Would you like another cup of coffee, Barbara?"

As they sipped their coffee in the living room, Peggy was quiet. Finally, Barbara stood up. "I guess I had a nerve to come here looking for your help. It really is an imposition. I saw you at the meeting and there was no chance for me to ask about applying during that melee. I saw your name on the mailboxes in the lobby and figured I'd try you. Can you at least point me in the right direction?"

Barbara started to walk toward the door.

Peggy put up her hands as if to stop her. "No, don't go. I think you might have important information, and I will try to help you. You don't strike me as a killer and I think you're in a nasty position. Here, have another cup of coffee while I get my notebook."

When she came back in the room, Peggy had a plate full of sliced, warm coffee cake she'd just taken from her new oven. Jack had gotten her the very special new stove she'd been wanting for her whole life, a stainless steel gas-powered Viking, complete with a contract with a gas company who would deliver the propane gas to them. Now, the baking-loving Peggy could cook to her heart's content again, with a gas stove instead of the electric in the unit, which she could not get used to. This was almost as good as her gas stove back in Brooklyn. Obviously, Jack realized she was having trouble adjusting to their new home and he was trying to make it easier.

She placed the coffee cake and some plates on her coffee table.

Barbara was clearly uncomfortable, sipping her coffee.

"Here," she offered, handing Barbara a printed form. "Just fill this out and I'll take it. We'll arrange for a credit check and I'm sure the Board will approve you, especially under the circumstances."

She continued, "Why don't you tell me what you know about Jenna," she heard herself say. Why did I say that? She moaned inwardly.

"We do have a morals clause in the application, and since you are a suspect, that could go against you. However," she drawled, "this is ridiculous and of course, you must stay and take care of your father."

Barbara sat down and filled out the one-page form.

Peggy looked at her. "I will try to help you, Barbara. At least I'll try to help you set the record straight. I'm not a detective but maybe we can discover who else had reason to want Jenna dead."

She opened her notepad. It was an electronic notepad.

"Now, you said Jenna was some kind of a nurse or nurse's aide in a nursing home in Georgia." She typed the information into her notepad. "You also said her maiden name was Wagner. Isn't that right?"

Barbara nodded. "The detective agency I hired told me that. They found that on the marriage license filed in the county. They were married by a judge. I'm going through the process, right now, of trying to have the marriage annulled, but because of the murder, my lawyer said they're trying to make sure I'm not just out to end any claim her heirs might have on the estate! Can you imagine that woman claiming my father's money as her estate!" Barbara nearly burst into tears.

"I don't really care about the money," she continued. "My father and I were estranged for the last few years. I was mad at him, but didn't realize he was slipping away into Alzheimer's. Even my mother felt awful about that and so she told me the truth about their divorce.

"None of that matters now. He was aware of what was happening to him and he put himself into the nursing home while he could still handle his affairs. One nurse there tracked me down and that's when I tried to re-connect with him. I was too late. Jenna was new there and obviously had a plan, a very successful plan."

"We need to know more about her," Peggy said. "You said she was new there. Do you know anything else about her? Where was she from? Where did she work before this? Who are her heirs?"

Barbara just shook her head.

"If she had a successful plan, as you said, and I think correctly from the sounds of how quickly she moved in on your father, then we need to know more about her. Where did she work before? Was she ever married before, and, did she have any children?

"You know," Peggy finished, "You can't travel right now, but I've a good mind to go up to Georgia and see what I can find out about her."

Barbara opened her capacious handbag and pulled out a sheaf of papers, clipped together with a giant binder clip. "Here are copies of the reports the detective agency gave me. She seems to have had no record, neither marriage nor employment, beyond her attending classes for her CNA. All they could find out was she was a perfect student, very capable and adept. They couldn't praise her enough. They said she was just a bored housewife who said she wanted to try her hand at a medical career."

"Exactly what is a CNA?" Peggy asked.

"I didn't know that either," Barbara replied. "It's a Certified Nursing Assistant."

"Must be something new since I went to college. We had a nursing school in my college and they were registered nurses, and there were practical nurses too. What is the training like for this CNA?" Peggy said as she flipped through the detective's report.

"Looks like five to seven weeks training is all it takes.

That's very interesting," Peggy said.

Barbara stood to leave. "I've taken enough of your time, Mrs. Murray. Let me know if there's anything else you need for me to stay with my father. I don't want to leave him alone, morals clause or not. I've called my husband and he'll be here this weekend."

Peggy saw her to the door. "Don't worry about staying here. I'll see to that for you. Let's hope the police finish this investigation quickly. Who else witnessed your outbursts with Jenna, beside Jerry Sands?"

Why did I stick my nose into this, Peggy thought.

"Well, his wife heard me yelling at them when I followed them to his apartment. He's in the dolphin building. They didn't know his wife was home. The stupid oaf complained to his wife right in front of us that she was supposed to be at a tennis tournament when she opened the door to find out what the commotion was all about. Can you imagine those two going to his place because she didn't want to go to hers, where my poor father was, alone and confused! I guess I'm lucky she didn't flaunt that idiot in my father's face."

"Oh that's awful!" Peggy exclaimed. "She was a horrid woman."

Peggy called Ralph and explained to him why she wanted Barbara and her husband cleared to move into the apartment with Walter Rivers. He agreed to clear the application, considering Peggy's conversation with Barbara as the interview.

Jack came home from his golf game and found Peggy busy at her computer. "What's got you so interested?" he said, bending to kiss her forehead.

"You won't believe what's happened today," she said. "It's been a very strange day, so far and it's only afternoon."

"Okay," Jack breathed out loud. "Want to do something later? I'm sorry about not going to the meeting with you, Peg. That was really not too nice of me. What would you like to do?" he said.

"How about dinner in Georgia, honey," she smiled up at him.

"Are you kidding?" he said back.

"Yes, I am. But, I would like to finish a little research and then go to the island for dinner."

Finally, Peggy closed her laptop down.

"I can't believe the shabby job that detective agency did," she said. "I found newspaper articles about her long-term marriage, her becoming a doctor, and losing her medical license. She was actually a medical doctor. I am surprised. I thought maybe she had a doctorate in underwater basket-weaving. And," she continued, "her ex husband was murdered and the murder was never solved."

"She was an anesthesiologist. She evidently over-dosed a patient. The thirty-nine year old man is now in a nursing home with the ability level of a four-year old. The lawsuit nearly broke the hospital where she worked and gave his wife millions. The wife lost it and had to be restrained, finally ending up in a mental ward."

Jack shook his head. "So much for minding our own business," he laughed. "Now, come on downstairs with me. I have a surprise for you," Jack said.

It was dusk and the sun was painting a beautiful sunset in the sky as Jack and Peggy emerged from the elevator on the ground floor level of the Manatee building. While it was very humid, the air was soft and smelled of one of Florida's beautiful flowers, the gardenia.

Peggy looked at her parking space and she fumed. "Look at that car! How does this person think I can get into my car? That car is so close to mine that I wouldn't even be able to open the driver's door. It's parked way over the line!"

"That's the car Herb and I were talking about. It's actually a Mustang but it's a very sporty model. It's got a six speed transmission." Jack said, smiling at the offending car. "Forget it. Maybe it's a snowbird and will be flying home soon."

"I don't care what kind of transmission it has or if its owner will be flying home soon. It's owner doesn't know how to park. I'm going to find out who it is and make my complaint official." Peggy said huffily. "If I had an emergency, I wouldn't be able to get my car out."

They were walking together toward the guest parking spaces.

Jack smiled at her. "Honey, you've been under too much stress. Finding a dead body isn't exactly what we came down here for. I know you're not really very happy here what with not having our own driveway and with transient friends. Also, I know you're bored to death. So I thought you should have a break.

"Instead of buying a place in New York so we can become snowbirds, I thought maybe we could try something different."

He stopped walking, took her arm in his right hand, and pointed to a very sleek RV parked across several guest parking spaces, against the rules of the Association.

Peggy followed his pointed finger and drew in her breath as she looked at a vehicle with "Dolphin" painted on its side.

She was speechless.

Jack said, "Want to have a look inside?" He started to walk toward the vehicle, Peggy walking with him.

"I wasn't really golfing all those times. When I skipped out on the meeting, I was shopping for this and I was learning how to drive it. "

Peggy nodded as Jack opened the door to the Dolphin and led her inside.

"I learned about how to find and reserve spots in all the camps around the country. We can even go to New York and visit the grandkids, and maybe our own children. If we want to see Lisa and her new husband, we can go without anyone having to put us up. We have room if we want to take a few of the older kids on a trip. If we don't like it, we'll return it and forget about it. What do you say, Peg?"

Peggy looked around the roomy and well appointed inside of the Dolphin. She walked swiftly through its passages, loved the kitchen and first bathroom she came to, noting the sleeping capacity of the two bedrooms. The hallway opened to what was, apparently, the master bedroom suite, the master bathroom being what they called "very updated and upscale".

"This will more than do," she exclaimed, turning to Jack, a huge smile on her face. "I love it. We'll have so much fun. You'll have to teach me how to drive it. What will we do with our cars?"

"Hold it," Jack laughed. "I can arrange to store your car and we'll trailer mine to use if we stay somewhere any length of time. We'll make the final arrangements after we plan out our first trip.

"I'm so glad you like the idea." Jack finished.

Someone watched the Murrays enter the Dolphin. "I could pick them both off right now if I wanted to. I'll see if it's necessary."

"I'm sorry I was so mad at you for not coming to the meeting with me," Peggy said as they left the RV and started walking across the parking lot toward their building.

"Well, how were you to know I wasn't just running off to play some more golf," he said, good-humoredly. "Look, there's your parking culprit getting into her car now," Jack said. "Now don't go at her, Peggy. She's an old woman."

"You're right, Jack," she said. "I wouldn't want to make trouble for Veronica. She's a very sweet old lady. Barbara told me she's been very kind to her since she came here to help her father. She had been helping him behind Jenna's back."

They had a wonderful dinner on the island at the Beach House. It was still early when they got home. Peggy was restless. She looked at the packet of papers Barbara had given her.

"I think I'll return these papers to Barbara. I'll tell her what I found out and then I'll be out of it," she said to Jack.

"Why are you bothering, Peg," he asked.

"I feel sorry for Barbara. I have to return these papers to her and I might at least tell her what I found out. That's really about all I can do. I think I'll also tell Detective de Leon what I found out. Actually, I'll type it up and e-mail it to her. I'll print it and bring it up to Barbara."

Barbara answered the door and was pleased to see Veronica waiting on the other side, a casserole in her hands. She offered the dish to Barbara and retrieved her standing cane.

"Please come in, Veronica," Barbara said. "This is so nice of you."

"I think you need a break from all the chaos around here," Veronica said and walked inside the apartment.

Peggy took the elevator down to the second floor, not feeling like taking the stairs at night since the lights on the staircase went out last week and were not replaced.

She walked over to the Rivers' apartment and knocked on the door. Barbara opened the door and beckoned Peggy inside.

"Oh, hello, Veronica. Nice to see you again." Peggy said on seeing Veronica sitting on the couch. "Am I interrupting?"

"No, No," Barbara said, smiling. "Veronica has been patiently listening to my complaints against Jenna. I really shouldn't be going on about her, after all, she is dead and I'm rid of her."

"Well, that's okay then," Peggy said. "I take it I can speak candidly about what I've found out about Jenna?"

"Absolutely," Barbara said.

"Well, I found a lot on line, once I had her maiden name, Jenna Wagner," Peggy began. When she finished she handed the copy of the printed detailed report she'd mailed to Detective Graham.

Barbara took the sheet of paper and was silent. Veronica shook her head as if in disbelief.

Finally, Barbara looked up at Peggy. "Why don't you sit down, Peggy. Have a cup of tea. I'm grateful for what you've done. I'll give this information to my lawyer. It might help him in dealing with the police on my behalf, but, I think, it will surely help me disengage her from my father's affairs."

Peggy sat down across from the two ladies on the couch. She seemed to be arguing with herself and finally made a decision.

"I think I'd better tell you something else. I already e-mailed this report to Detective de Leon. When I saw that Jenna's ex-husband was murdered, and also by a sniper's hand, and it's unsolved, I thought I should let her know what I'd found out. She might have already known most of it."

Feeling uncomfortable, Peggy stood up to leave, having turned down the offer of tea. Why am I so uncomfortable she thought. I shouldn't have spoken. I should have just given Barbara the report and left.

Veronica smiled at her, to Peggy's relief. "Now that I have you here," Veronica said, "whatever happened to Miss Claudia? I didn't want to seek you out over such nonsense, but I wondered if she was in jail or the hospital."

"Well, she is a concern because of her episodes. However, when she's on her meds, she's really a very nice and interesting person. She's home now. The hospital got her back on her meds and arranged for a caregiver to monitor her for a while. I'd better get back to Jack. I promised him I'd be back early."

"Yes," Veronica said. "I guess you two have a lot to talk about tonight. I saw the beautiful RV you have. Are you planning a trip?"

Peggy started toward the door. "Well, I was thinking of a little trip up to Georgia to follow Jenna Wagner's trail. I became intrigued when I realized she was a Bradenton native but didn't seem to have any friends here. The fact that her husband, I mean her ex-husband, was murdered the same way, and it is still unsolved, is very strange. I think it will let you off the hook, Barbara.

"Good night, all. I have to be up early tomorrow. The aqua exercise class is taking over my usual morning swim time so I'm going down early."

Peggy tossed and turned all night. When she awoke at quarter past three, she tried to organize her thoughts to see if that would put her mind to rest so she could get some sleep.

Maybe Barbara isn't as decent as she seems. It isn't likely that the private detective she hired to find her father didn't tell her more than she says. If I could find all that about Jenna on the internet, why wouldn't a professional investigator be able to do at least what I did? She asked herself. I don't want to be taken in by Barbara because I feel sorry for her. She's also from Georgia as is the murdered ex-husband.

What about Kathryn Sands? Her husband made a fool of her in front of this whole complex. Maybe she lost it.

How about Jerry himself? I saw him on the pool deck the night she was killed. Why was she drugged, or "rufied" as they say on the street. I saw him spill something in her glass before I saw them on the pool deck. Why did he do that? She asked herself. At least she had reported that to Detective de Leon.

The question is, she finally realized. Which one of them knows how to shoot a sniper rifle? They all have motives but, is it possible they all know how to shoot?

That settled her mind and she fell into a deep sleep.

Chapter Ten:
Let Me Think About This

Peggy decided she needed to go for her eight o'clock swim at seven this morning. She had searched everywhere she could on her computer in her pursuit of Jenna Wagner Rivers' past. Prior to her securing her CNA Certificate and subsequent employment in the very expensive Saint Anselm Nursing Home, she had been a doctor. Now, she decided, that when she returned from the pool, she would research the others in this case.

I might as well admit it, she thought. I'm going to look into this. I need to know if I'm living in a small community with a murderer hiding here.

Peggy didn't even look at her computer this morning, preferring a glass of orange juice and a quick run to the pool. It was already after seven and if she didn't get her hour in before the aqua class, she would be off all day.

I wonder if I'm OCD, she thought. I never understood about Obsessive Compulsive Disorder until the last few years of my teaching career. All those professional development courses were so helpful. Thank goodness we're able to understand these things now. Some of the children we taught before we understood these disorders really suffered. We thought they just didn't want to do their work.

She missed teaching.

She got into the heated pool at ten minutes after seven. The warm waters felt so comforting to Peggy's tense and tired body. She followed her routine, first floating on the noodles and then going into her laps.

The routine allowed her to think.

Kathryn Sands took her coffee out to the lanai and looked down at the pool. It looked so nice in the rising sun. The lake sparkled beyond the pool. She sat and looked at the brightening sky as the sun rose, almost suddenly. The sky was showing a blazing scene of reds and golds against the darkest blue of the earlier moment. It was as if a light switch was turned on.

Detective de Leon drove to the Sea Grass Condominium Complex. There was no traffic this morning. She was grateful. If Emily Watkins is at that complex, she was thinking, and if she knows Peggy Murray is digging into her business, Peggy will either be shot or have an accident. Her sense of urgency was tangible.

Peggy relaxed. Miss Claudia is back and the sky is falling. What foolish nonsense. They're all nervous because Miss Claudia is back from the hospital. She's a lot of huff and puff but she really doesn't do all that harm. Unless pushing Mable down on the floor is very harmful. She laughed inwardly at the memory of Mable's shock at finding herself on the floor. Poor Kathryn. I'd be so embarrassed if I had such a wussy husband.

Barbara has a good motive for wanting Jenna dead, but she's not a killer. How about the unsolved murder of Jenna's ex-husband in Georgia! That has to be connected to Jenna's murder. Both of them shot by a sniper? Doesn't sound like Barbara or Kathryn. Not even Jerry.

Stupid Jerry Sands didn't do it. He probably doesn't know how to shoot a gun any more than I do. He's certainly not my candidate as being an accomplished sniper. He's just a cheater.

She was on her last lap. Her memory jumped to the previous evening and she visualized Veronica getting into her Mustang that afternoon. I don't care if she parks too close to my car anymore. I can't keep letting little things bother me.

But, her sudden thought, alarmed her. How can someone as lame as Veronica drive a six speed manual shift? She can't. And I detected a slight Georgian drawl in Veronica's soft voice. All of us talk about where we're from, but Veronica never says. There's a Georgia plate on her car.

Peggy turned on her back to back stroke to the ladder. She saw a shadow running across the pool deck.

Kathryn watched in horror as she saw Veronica toss her cane and pick up the boom box. Moments before she had seen Mable Milano plug in that same box for the morning aerobics class. She ran to her screen door and opened it so she could get to her railing.

"Veronica!" she called. "Don't you dare…Peggy get out of that pool." Veronica was heading to the edge of the pool, the boom box lifted high above her head.

Peggy was scrambling to get on the metal ladder to get out of the pool. She was closer to the ladder than to the pool steps.

Suddenly, Veronica was face down on the deck of the pool. A triumphant Mable Milano sitting on her and holding the precious boom box on her lap.

"What are you," Mable yelled at Veronica, "some kind of nut? Were you trying to kill Peggy and ruin our boom box at the same time?"

Mable started to cry.

Peggy ran over to her. "Mabel! Thank you. You saved my life!"

"I was afraid she'd ruin our boom box."

By now Kathryn Sands had made it to the pool. "Oh thank God for Mable. I couldn't believe my eyes when I saw what was happening down here."

"Well, I heard you yell and got to the ladder as fast as I could. I saw her getting ready to toss the boom box into the pool and I felt like my swimming was not fast enough. It seemed to take me forever to get to the ladder."

Mable looked at Peggy. "What am I going to do? I can't just sit on her and I think she's too strong for me if I let her up. This is no sweet old lady. Is it Claudia in disguise?" Mable was shrieking and crying at the same time.

Then Miss Claudia seemed to come out of nowhere. "You're all too stupid to know what to do. I'd feed her to the alligators if I was in charge here."

Jack had joined the unlikely foursome. "What in the world is happening here!" he said.

"Just an attempted murder of your wife," Claudia said, smiling broadly. "Too bad it failed because of this loudmouth Mable. That's what I'll call you from now on. Loudmouth Mable."

"You stop that this instant," Peggy said, putting her arm protectively around Mable's shoulders. "Mable saved my life, Jack. That's what's happening."

Mable gave a quick snort, and said, "I only acted because Kathryn's screams alerted me When I saw what she was doing, I was sure it was Miss Claudia trying to kill Peggy and destroy our boom box." She sobbed again.

Detective de Leon arrived at the pool deck and immediately called for backup.

"How did you get here so quickly," Jack asked.

"I couldn't sleep last night after I'd opened your e-mail," she said to Peggy. "The fact that Jenna's ex-husband had also been shot by a sniper, and it remained unsolved, made me think, it couldn't be a coincidence. I thought Jenna's patient's wife had a better motive than anyone here at the complex for wanting to kill her. Evidently, she was released from the mental ward and decided to kill Jenna's husband to get back at her."

As they were handcuffing Veronica, detective de Leon said, "Allow me to introduce you to Emily Watkins, the wife of Seymour Watkins. He's the patient who cost Doctor Jenna Rivers her medical license and her ex-husband his life."

"Yes", screamed the now handcuffed woman formerly known as Veronica. "Then I found out she was no longer married to that drunken fool so I had to go after her. I was going to kill her second husband, but I couldn't hurt her by doing that. She didn't care a whit about him. So she had to go herself.

"You know, Peggy, you just had to get into my business. I could have shot you easily, but I wanted it to look like an accident."

The officers took her away.

Mable finally stopped crying.

Peggy went over to her. "Why don't we sit down and have a cop of coffee, Mable. We can all have a cup on my lanai."

Jack nodded. "I already put the pot on, ladies. Come on up."

Kathryn helped Mable to her feet and she sniffled all the way up to the Murray's apartment and halfway through to their coffee Klatch on the lanai.

They heard the aerobics class down on the pool deck.

"Oh, no!" Mable cried. "I have to go down and plug in the boom box for the class. It's my job."

Peggy said, "I think the police seized it for evidence."

It was almost dusk. Jack put his arm around Peggy. "Do you still want to drive up to Georgia, Peg" he said.

"No. I think that's not necessary now. Maybe I'd like to do something that isn't necessary. I have to learn that everything I do doesn't have to be necessary. I've been thinking a lot about retirement and not doing things because they're necessary."

"You think of something and I'll pack us what we need to take on our RV," she smiled, satisfied with herself.

"I think I have just the place for us to roam. I'll take care of your car in the morning if you'll pack a few things, maybe for two weeks, and include some warm clothes. You know, the works. Raingear, snow gear, whatever." Jack said.

"It's a deal. I'll even pack some food. By the way," she asked, "what do you think happened to the Andersons?'

Jack laughed. "Maybe we should make it our business to find out."

The End

www.ingramcontent.com/pod-product-compliance
Lightning Source LLC
Chambersburg PA
CBHW071232130726
47998CB00003B/925